FANG GANG

CYN

This year has not been easy, so for the first time, I dedicate this book to ME. I am so proud of myself for pushing through 🤍

CONTENTS

DATING A VAMPIRE WAS EMPOWERING. Fallon loved that shit and the respect it earned her. Of course, her peers had no idea that vampires were real, but that didn't matter. People could feel that power. Whenever her nigga stepped foot in a room, respect was commanded. Nobody tried him, and everyone either wanted to be him, or to be with him.

As she sat on the stone ledge outside of the University of New Orleans, where she attended college, Fallon wasn't ignorant of the small crowd gathering several feet away from her. It happened every day, Monday through Thursday, when she had class. They were doing the same thing she was... waiting for her man, Kendrick, to show up.

Fallon rolled her eyes as the bitches fell over themselves to get the best angle while the niggas stood back, trying to act like they weren't there to catch a glimpse of her boyfriend, too. She leaned back some on the concrete, placing her hands behind her for support as she tilted her head up to the sun, soaking that shit up. It was hot as hell in New Orleans that day, and Fallon loved it. Her ginger hair hung down her back in long waves, and her melanin skin seemed to glow under the bright rays. The gold hoop nose ring in her septum caught the light, and she smiled slightly at the breeze.

A horn honking startled her out of the peaceful moment. Her eyes popped open, and her grin was immediate. She heard the fan club giggling as he got out of the car, but she tuned them out as she hopped up and grabbed her black Birkin bag. Black was her favorite color. All black everything was her daily attire, and that day was no different. Her black red bottoms snapped against the concrete as she made her way over to her man, who was now holding the door open for her. She added a little extra sway to her hips, already knowing her black skinny jeans formed to her Coke bottle shape flawlessly. The black body-suit she wore accentuated her big breasts and sat snuggly over her snatched waist. She knew she was the shit, but when her nigga looked at her like the only woman in the world, much like he was doing now, it made her big ass head grow.

Fallon walked right into his big frame and

wrapped her arms around his waist as she tilted her head, resting her chin just below his pecks, looking up at him.

"Hey, Beauty," he said smoothly as he looked down at her. His New Orleans accent was thick, and she loved that shit. She was born and raised here, so normally it wouldn't faze her, but with Kendrick it was different. His voice did something to her every single time.

Fallon purred, "I missed you."

He tilted his head back and laughed, his fangs gleaming in the sun for just a moment before he closed his mouth again. Fallon was the only person in the world that could pull a smile out of him, let alone a laugh, which meant his fangs were easily hidden from the world. It didn't matter, though. The gang wore gold fronts melded to their teeth to cover that shit up. Gold fang grills were in right now, so it was a no-brainer, and people didn't think much of it.

Fallon's eyes crinkled as she looked up at him, loving the way the sun hit his dark skin. She was glad the whole theory about the sun killing vampires wasn't true, because if it was, there was no way she would have ever met Kendrick Danger. He would probably live in Alaska or some shit, not down south where the sun didn't seem to stop. Contrary to popular belief, the sun was actually a vampire's friend. It helped warm their cold blood. Believe it or not, the cold was a vampire's enemy. Too much cold and a vampire could find themselves frozen in time until someone moved them to a warm climate. If nobody ever did, they would just stay that way for an eternity. Not dead, just frozen. Apparently, the shit was excruciating, too.

"I just saw you this morning," Kendrick responded.

She nodded. "You did, but you know I hate being away from you, bae."

"I know," he replied, bending down and kissing her nose. "Wit' yo' clingy ass."

Fallon bit her full bottom lip, but didn't respond because it was true. She loved being up under her man.

Kendrick chuckled and nudged her toward the inside of the car. She got the hint and slid in. It took no time for him to slide into the driver's seat, and before he put the car in drive, he leaned over and kissed Fallon on the lips.

"You ready?" he asked when he pulled back.

"Always, baby," she replied, putting her seatbelt on and settling into the buttery seats. Fallon watched in the rearview mirror as her peers tripped over themselves to watch the car disappear.

Pathetic, Fallon thought. She knew her nigga was

the shit, but there was no way she would ever come off so thirsty. It was probably what drew Kendrick to her in the first place. They met at a club one night not too far from campus. Fallon was with some classmates, but she was never one to stick with the crowd. She had been dancing by herself in the middle of the dance floor when Kendrick slid up to her. She was completely unbothered by him. On the outside, at least. On the inside, she was just as weak to him as every other bitch. He loved that shit and had been chasing after her ever since, even after he got her.

"How was class?" Kendrick asked, pulling Fallon's gaze from the window as he lifted her hand and kissed the back of it.

"Long as hell. That history class is kicking my ass, as usual. I don't know why I decided to take that shit as an elective, anyway. I hate history," Fallon grumbled.

"How can you hate history when you're dating a vampire that's a thousand years old?" Kendrick chuckled.

Fallon gave him the side-eye. "You make history interesting. Hearing about shit from hundreds of years ago from someone that was there is dope as fuck, which was why my happy ass decided to take the class in the first place, but it's nowhere near as interesting as when you talk about it, so really, I have you to blame."

Kendrick chuckled and said, "You'll be alright. You're the smartest woman I know."

Fallon let out a loud sigh and turned in her seat, so she was fully facing her man. With a devilish grin, she said, "Bae, you should teach that class. People would learn so much more, and they would actually retain the information coming from your fine ass."

Kendrick shook his head. "Been there, done that, baby. My teaching days are over. Besides, your lil' ass wouldn't learn a thing if I was up in your face all day."

He flashed his fangs, and Fallon melted back into her seat. Of course, he had been a professor. There wasn't much of anything Kendrick hadn't done. How could he not? He was nine hundred and fifty-six years old. He'd lived dozens of lifetimes. Anyone would get bored enough to try everything at least once. Fallon marveled at him as she sat back and watched him handle the luxury car with ease. He was too damn fine with his mocha skin and amber eyes. His big lips curved up, so it looked like he was always smirking, and his hair was faded on the sides with dreads that were long and twisted, pulled into a man bun at the top. The full, long beard was what really did it for her. Sexy as fuck.

"You're right." Fallon giggled.

She pried her eyes from Kendrick's God-like face and settled in for the ride to The Lair. It was a good forty-five-minute drive, one that Kendrick happily made two times a day on the days Fallon had class. She was his baby, and since her parents were dead, her grandmother who raised her wasn't speaking to her, and she had no siblings, Kendrick and the gang were all she had.

She smiled a little as she thought about The Fang Gang, or TFG, as they called themselves. They were her crew. Her people. Since it was a Friday, she knew sleep wouldn't come anytime soon once she stepped foot through The Lair, so she rested her head on the cool window and closed her eyes, intent on catching a quick nap before her night began.

"THERE'S OUR GIRL," Papa shouted, jumping down from the second floor banister and landing gently on his feet as soon as Kendrick and Fallon entered the mansion known as The Lair. Papa grasped Fallon around the waist and pulled her from Kendrick's arms and into his own.

Fallon laughed as Papa slow danced with her, whirling her around the grand foyer and then dipping her low.

"Are you drunk already, Papa?" Fallon asked, as her feet tried to keep up with his movements.

Papa didn't miss a beat. He kept leading her around the room with a wistful look on his face. "Call me Beyonce, baby, because I'm drunk and in love."

"Again?" Kendrick groaned as he snapped his arm out and snatched Fallon, who was becoming dizzy, right out of Papa's arms. He steadied her and grinned down at her before cutting his eyes at Papa, waiting for an explanation.

"This time it really is true love," Papa replied with a gleam in his eyes.

Fallon looked up at Kendrick with worry in her own eyes, but she knew better than to voice her opinion. It never got her anywhere with these unruly vamps. She did, however, feel bad for the poor soul who caught Papa's eye. Pablo was his real name, but everyone called him Papa. He was a hopeless romantic and desperate to find his mate. He even had more options because he was open to both men and women. Fallon would have fed into his love schemes if there wasn't one slight problem. Vampires could only turn humans who were their fated mates, which essentially made them one through the mating bond. If the human they chose to turn wasn't their fated mate, then the human died after they were bitten. Sometimes, a vampire was lucky enough to have several mates, and sometimes, there was only one. A lot of vampires opted out of trying altogether, and some were mated on an accidental feed gone wrong.

The thing was, vampires actually had a lot of control when it came to feeding on humans. The only time they drained them was if they wanted to kill them, or if they wanted to mate to them. Papa had killed hundreds upon hundreds of humans in his quest to find true love. Story had it that back in the 60s, he went a bit crazy and bit every human he came by in order to find his mate. Fallon found it sad that so many people had to die at the hands of Papa, who was otherwise the sweetest creature she had ever met. She wished he would find his person so his killing sprees could stop. She knew the guilt weighed on him heavily, and she also knew it was the reason he no longer took the time out to truly get to know his conquests. It had to be a heavy burden to kill people he grew to love, only to find out they weren't his to keep.

"Okay," Kendrick replied, guiding Fallon toward the grand staircase that led to the second floor of The Lair, which was really just a big ass ominous mansion away from the city. "You have fun with that."

"I will," Papa sang as he twirled around. "He's coming over tonight."

Kendrick shook his head and continued up the stairs with Fallon on his heels. Once they were on the second floor and down the hall, away from Papa's super vamp hearing, Fallon whispered, "Does he have to do that here?"

Kendrick opened the door to their bedroom and ushered her inside. Once the door was closed, he replied, "I know you hate it, but there really is no safer place for him to do it. It's messier doing it in a public place when we can just do it here for an easy cleanup."

Fallon shuddered. She knew human life didn't mean quite as much to them as it did to her, but to hear her boyfriend talk about someone's murder so nonchalantly would always be chilling to her.

Fallon walked over to the king-sized bed with the four gold posts, dropped her school bag and purse, and then flopped down. "Yeah. I know."

In a flash, Kendrick was at her side. She grinned at his super-speed and nuzzled into him when he pulled her into his lap. He kissed the top of her head and said, "How about we skip out on the partying tonight? We can hole up in here and watch movies... or not watch them."

His suggestive tone made Fallon giggle, but she was thankful for his offer. She knew he was giving her a way out of seeing the poor man that would fall victim to Papa's love quest. Seeing their faces was always hard for her. "You know Scarlette isn't going for that."

"Let me handle her," he murmured in her ear.

"Thank you, baby," Fallon replied, relieved that she could sit this one night out. She loved partying as much as the next girl, but not when death was looming. Besides, she knew there would always be tomorrow night, and that was sure to be the more wild night out of the two. Whenever Papa failed to turn a mate, he partied. Hard. Like a good friend, Fallon would be there to cheer him up and take tequila shots with him until they both passed out. She never held their vampire ways against them. It took some time, but she worked hard to understand that everything they did was in their nature. She realized they really were gentle souls once she got past that, but at the same time, she knew they kept the real murder shit away from her. They weren't called The Fang Gang for nothing. They'd been rolling together for centuries and were notorious in the vampire community. Fallon wasn't stupid. She knew it was because they were ruthless, or at least had been back in the day, but she didn't want to know too much about that part of her family. As far as she was concerned, the fewer murders she knew about, the better.

"Why don't you get in the shower, and I'll go talk to Scarlette and Axel. Think about what you want for dinner, and I'll order once you're done, okay?"

"Can I choose the movie, too?" Fallon asked, batting her eyelashes up at him.

He sighed dramatically. "Fine, but no vampire shit. I'm serious, Fallon."

One of her favorite things to do was to watch

vampire shows or movies and compare how much of the information they got right and what was terribly wrong. Since finding out about vampires four years ago, she'd been obsessed with the fact that she knew this big secret, while nobody else around her did.

"Fine, baby. I got you. No vampire shit. You have my word." She giggled as she rolled off the bed and walked into the massive bathroom attached to the room, knowing she was lying her ass off.

While she got undressed and turned on the hot water, she thought back to the day Kendrick told her he was a vampire. There hadn't been some big revelation, nor had the news really shocked her too much. Somewhere deep inside, she just understood and took it in stride. Her willingness to accept that vampires were real had shocked Kendrick, but for some reason, it just felt right to her. They'd been dating for six months at that point, and afterward, Kendrick told her he was nervous she would leave him after he told her what he was, but she laughed it off, telling him he was still the same nigga she was falling in love with. Secretly, she felt like those words, and her willingness to accept him for what he was, were the reasons he loved her so much. The nigga loved her so much he refused to attempt to turn her. Honestly, Fallon was okay with that. She didn't truly want to be a vampire, but she knew there might come a time where her love for Kendrick would overpower her desire to live and die as a human, and when that happened, she knew she would have to revisit the conversation with her man.

She finally stepped into the water once the temperature was to her liking, and she made quick work of cleaning her body before getting out and drying off. She rubbed lavender scented lotion all over herself before wrapping the towel securely around her chest and walking back into the bedroom.

"Bae—"

She was cut off when she was tackled to the ground. All she saw was a flurry of long, dark curls and gold fangs before she let out a scream.

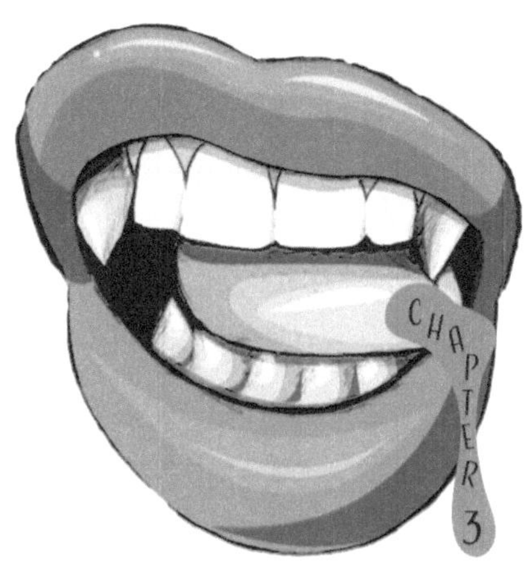

FALLON'S SCREAM quickly morphed into a loud laugh as Scarlette wrestled with her playfully. Still, Kendrick was in the room no more than one second later, always the protector. Fallon caught sight of him while Scarlette playfully nipped at her, and she laughed even harder.

"I'm sorry, bae," Fallon cried, as she tried wiggling from under Scarlette. "She startled me, is all. I'm fine."

Seconds later, Papa and Axel were filing into the room as well. All the vamps came running when the human girl screamed. Kendrick let out a breath and said, "Scarlette, get off my girl."

Scarlette relented and stood to her feet, finally allowing Fallon to catch her breath. She flung her long jet-black curls over her shoulder and said, "My bad. Fallon just has me fucked up, is all."

Before Fallon could blink, Kendrick was at her side and helping her up from the floor. Fallon adjusted the towel, making sure none of her goodies were showing, before she landed her eyes back on Scarlette. "How in the hell do I have you fucked up?"

Scarlette, a petite light skinned vamp with curls that touched her ass and emerald green eyes, pouted up her full lips and gazed at Fallon. "Because… you don't love me."

Going along with Scarlette's theatrics, Fallon crossed her arms over her towel covered chest and asked, "How do you figure that, Scar?"

"Yo' nigga just told me so," Scarlette pouted, jabbing a finger in Kendrick's direction.

Kendrick looked at Scarlette crazily while Fallon asked, "Bae, why did you tell her that?"

"I didn't, man. You know she's dramatic. I told her ass we weren't going to party tonight. That's what the fuck I said," he replied calmly.

"Same thing," Scarlette quipped with a shrug, her piercing eyes landing back on Fallon. "Just take one shot with me?"

"Uh uh," Fallon replied, followed by a giggle. "You know, once I get started, I don't stop."

"I know." Scarlette smiled brightly. "That's the point."

"Not tonight, sis. Tomorrow, I promise," Fallon

replied, her eyes flicking subtly over to Papa and back to Scarlette.

Scarlette's eyes softened, and she nodded her head slightly. Fallon knew her best friend understood her reasoning for flaking on the party tonight. "Fine… but tomorrow you owe me."

"I got you, babe. Now, can you all get out so I can get dressed?" Fallon asked, eying everyone else.

"Wait, you really aren't going to party tonight? You know tonight could be the night," Papa sang dreamily as he looked at Fallon with hope filled eyes, completely oblivious to her need to stay far away from the party.

"Not tonight, Papa," Fallon replied kindly.

Luckily, Papa was too much in lala land to put up much of a fight. "Fine. You can meet him tomorrow, then."

"Tomorrow," Fallon agreed halfheartedly, knowing it wasn't likely she would be meeting anyone the next day.

Scarlette looped her arm through Papa's and said, "Come on. Let's go choose your outfit for tonight. I'm thinking vintage chic."

Papa clapped his hands excitedly. "Oh, yes, baby! Let me raid your closet!"

Before Scarlette could object, he was out of the

room. She was only a second behind him, shouting for him to get out of her room.

Fallon shook her head and giggled before turning her attention to Axel. He and Scarlette were so similar in looks. His light skin matched hers perfectly, and those green eyes were piercing. The only difference was his face was a bit more angular, and his black curls were cropped close to his head.

Axel was Kendrick's right hand and his best friend. He was also Scarlette's twin brother, older by a few minutes. Kendrick was actually the one to turn Axel in the 1700s. Axel was the one and only human Kendrick ever attempted to turn, and he promised he would never do it again. The two met at the height of the Bubonic Plague in France. Kendrick had been a loner for many years, aside from the occasional visit from his parents, and he and Axel hit it off. They became more like brothers, but when Axel got the plague and was on his deathbed, Kendrick couldn't fathom the idea of going an eternity without his friend. That was how deep their bond had become in such a short amount of time. Kendrick ended up confiding in Axel about what he truly was. Axel, delirious with illness, asked Kendrick to turn him. After all, what was the worst that could happen? He was dying, anyway.

Kendrick bit him with a great deal of hesitance,

and when Axel didn't change right away, he lived with the guilt of killing his only friend for three whole days. He didn't fully know the process to change a vampire since he had never attempted it before. Sometimes, they woke right away, sometimes, they took a few days. The true sign it worked, they learned down the line, was if the person was still breathing after the bite.

Kendrick had been astonished because he and Scarlette, who traveled from Spain to see about her dying brother but was too late by the time she got there, buried him and were grieving together when Axel showed up alive, well, and a vampire.

Not okay with being the only mortal one in their newfound trio, Scarlette finally convinced Axel to change her, completely convinced it would work since she knew in her heart her brother *was* her heart. There was no way they wouldn't be eligible for the mating process, and she was correct. Ever since then, they'd been moving together, picking up Papa many years later along the way. The core members, Kendrick, Axel, Scarlette, and Papa, always remained. They were gang for life. They had other vamps through the years that came into the gang and went peacefully. They weren't on that Death Row shit where once niggas were gang, they could only leave in a body bag… nah. TFG didn't do shit like that.

There was only one rule to leave the gang peacefully… the member leaving could never betray them in any way. That meant talking shit or snitching about anything they may have seen while kickin' it with the gang. If word got around that someone was going against TFG, niggas would be chillin' in the North Pole before they could fully grasp what was happening. Luckily, that shit had yet to happen in all this time because niggas knew the deal, and they understood how lethal the gang was.

Other than that, TFG was extremely chill, and there wasn't even a brutal initiation into the gang. They just had to take an oath. No being blessed in, jumped in, or none of that shit. Stay loyal, and niggas could stay down. With that said, not everyone could be gang. It was actually very rare that someone was deemed good enough to kick it with the gang, let alone be initiated. Fallon was blessed in on the strength of Kendrick, but she wasn't technically gang because she wasn't a vampire. Still, they took her in as their own, which was why Axel had come running when he heard her screams.

"You good, sis?" Axel asked as he looked Fallon in the eyes.

He was normally jovial and the glue that kept the gang together when niggas were at odds, which happened often because every single one of them were stubborn and hardheaded as hell, but Axel got serious as hell when it came to the safety of the gang. He was like the security of the crew, even though none of them really needed security aside from Fallon. He was just the most calculating and observant out of them all, and his smile would fall the second he saw some shit that was looking funny. His protective side came out, and that shit was deadly when it needed to be, so Fallon flashed him a smile, and replied, "Stand down, killa. You know your sister loves fuckin' with me. That's all that was."

His eyes took one last sweep of the room before he nodded and looked at Kendrick. "I'll make sure these niggas leave y'all alone tonight. Enjoy your time together."

Before Fallon or Kendrick could reply, Axel was out of the room, leaving them alone. Kendrick walked over to the bed and flopped down on it before turning his head and gazing at Fallon, who was still standing in the middle of the room, holding her towel to her chest.

"You ever think about getting our own place?" he asked with a crooked smile.

Fallon barked out a laugh and shook her head. "Not a chance. You know it's gang for life. I can't imagine a house with just the two of us."

Kendrick repositioned, so he was leaned up on

one elbow. "What about when we have kids? You really want them around these crazy mothafuckas?"

Fallon looked at him like he was crazy. "Now you know we ain't going to have no damn kids. It's impossible unless I become a vampire. We can't procreate while I'm human, bae."

Vampire babies were a real thing, but this wasn't *Twilight*. There was no way possible for her to get pregnant while she was human and he was a vampire.

Before Fallon could blink, Kendrick was up and holding her in his arms with her legs wrapped around his waist. She was almost dizzy with how fast he moved. It was something she had yet to get used to, even after four years.

"We can always adopt," he replied, nuzzling his nose into her neck.

Fallon pulled away with a giggle and peered into his dark eyes. "And what happens when I continue getting older and Daddy stays young forever? *They* will get older and eventually look older than you. How's that going to work? Will you mentally be able to handle losing your entire family?"

Kendrick thought about it for a split second before saying, "We could find some vampire kids to adopt."

Fallon raised one eyebrow at him. "Oh, so I'll be the only one to die?"

"How about this?" Kendrick propositioned before running them over to the bed with his vamp speed and plopping them both down so he was lying on top of her. "How about we just practice making babies for now?"

He kissed her neck, and Fallon giggled before flipping over so she was on top of him. She leaned down to kiss him sensually before pulling away. "Bet, but let's wait until the party starts. You know we can get a bit loud, and I'm not trying to hear anyone's mouths tomorrow about this shit."

Kendrick groaned when she stood up. He instantly missed the pressure her hot ass pussy was putting on his dick when she was on top of him. "Bae, they have vamp hearing. They'll hear us, regardless."

Fallon knew that was true, but it didn't make it any less embarrassing.

"Humor me," she replied before turning on her heels and sauntering toward the walk-in closet so she could throw on some biker shorts and a baby tee before cuddling up with her man for the night.

A FEW HOURS PASSED, and Fallon could hear the bass below them as music blasted and the occasional cheer or shout from the partygoers. Fallon was lying on Kendrick's chest in a food coma, watching *The Vampire Diaries*.

"I just love Klaus," Fallon said, as she mindlessly drew circles on Kendrick's chest.

"He ain't shit but a knockoff white version of me," Kendrick grumbled. He hated watching these shows because they were completely inaccurate, and Fallon easily fell in love with fictional characters. He wasn't the jealous type at all. He just marveled at how she could love these fictional vampires when he could do most of the shit they could, but better.

"Awe, what's wrong, stink?" Fallon teased as she leaned up and pecked Kendrick on the lips. "You know there is no other vamp out there for me."

She nuzzled into his neck, and Kendrick grabbed her around the waist before flipping her over so he was on top of her once again. "Keep that Klaus nigga's name out yo' mouth then, *stink*."

Fallon giggled, and Kendrick leaned back some so he could watch her. She was truly beautiful in his eyes, and he was madly in love with her. Times like these were when he wanted to freeze time. He was a strong mothafucka, but that was one power he didn't have. His heart ached slightly at the thought of one day losing Fallon, but before he could spiral down that rabbit hole, Fallon grabbed his face in both of her petite hands and forced him to look her in her emerald eyes. "Stop it."

She knew her man well enough to know where his head had gone just now, and she wasn't for that shit. Fallon was a firm believer that she had to cherish each moment and live in them to the fullest. Worrying about the future or stressing over the past did nothing but diminish what was right in front of her. It was something she was desperately trying to teach Kendrick, and with her help, he was easily able to snap back into reality and enjoy the here and now.

He gave her a soft smile before gently pressing his lips into hers. When he pulled back, he cocked his head to the side and asked, "Do you hear that?"

"What?" Fallon asked as she strained her ears to

hear whatever it was Kendrick was inquiring about. Her hearing wasn't anywhere near as good as his, so she easily grew frustrated and gave up with trying to figure out what Kendrick was talking about.

Kendrick smiled down at her with a devilish grin, showcasing his gold covered fangs. "The party is in full swing, and I believe you promised me something earlier…"

"I don't recall making any promises," Fallon quipped, playing along with Kendrick. Her pussy instantly became moist as she prepared herself for what was to come. Sex with Kendrick was magical. She hadn't been a virgin when they got together, but she may as well have been because she realized quickly that she knew absolutely nothing about her body or pleasure until she met him.

"Let me help you remember," Kendrick murmured against her lips.

As a response, Fallon wrapped her legs around his waist and pulled him closer. That gave Kendrick the green light to kick things up a notch, so he slid his tongue inside her mouth. Fallon moaned and flicked her tongue over his gold fangs gently. They were sharp as hell, and the last thing she wanted to do was accidentally cut herself on them.

Kendrick pulled away slightly when her tongue

flicked across his fangs, and Fallon grinned against his lips. "Relax, bae."

"You know I worry about hurting you," he replied.

Fallon shook her head. "You won't."

Kendrick didn't respond. He knew he would never intentionally hurt her, but he often felt Fallon didn't realize just how strong he was and how much restraint he had to practice when dealing with her. She was much more fragile than she realized, and he knew she loved his fangs, but he always pulled away when she got too close to them. He was very careful with who he tried to turn. He always had been. It was why he only turned Axel, mostly because he had seen firsthand the agony that was caused when attempting to turn someone he loved went wrong.

Instead of responding to Fallon, Kendrick pulled her shirt and shorts off before she could even blink and tossed them on the floor. Fallon tugged at his t-shirt, and he quickly pulled it over his head before reaching down and discarding his pants and boxers.

Fallon moaned in anticipation at the weight of his dick pressed against her stomach. "I want you, baby."

Kendrick normally took his time with her. He loved eating Fallon's pussy and kissing every inch of her body, driving her into insanity with the need for him to fill her, but tonight, he felt that need without barely even touching her. He slid his finger down into her slippery folds, and it amazed him at how wet she already was.

"I been craving you all day," Fallon whispered as he slid a finger into her.

"You could have had me hours ago," Kendrick said as he worked his finger in and out of her.

Fallon shook her head as she tried to keep up with the conversation. With only his fingers, he was on the brink of driving her insane. "I told you… I didn't… want anyone… to hear us, bae."

She was panting, and Kendrick gave her his signature lopsided grin. "Scary ass."

Fallon would have responded, but Kendrick pulled his finger out of her and replaced it with his dick. Her back automatically arched, and a gasp fell out of her lips while Kendrick groaned, "Shit."

She wound her hips to match his pace, and he reached under her with one large hand and grabbed her ass so he could go as deep as possible. Fallon felt as though she couldn't breathe, but in the best possible ways. What felt like a storm was brewing in her lower abdomen, and she braced herself because she knew what was next.

"You're about to cum on this dick, huh?"

Kendrick asked as he slowly stroked her into oblivion.

"Like you need to ask," Fallon breathed.

Kendrick smirked. She was right, for more reasons than one. All original vampires had an ability. Kendrick's was foresight. He knew shit that was going to happen before it did. It wasn't full proof. He couldn't pick and choose what he saw. He could typically only see shit that surrounded the people he was really in tune with or physically surrounded by, but sometimes he would get a strong sense of the future from niggas he never met that were trying to kill him. He could see that shit coming from a mile away, which saved him more times than he could count. He did, however, practice discretion with his gift. Although he could sense the future for himself and others around him, he did his best not to project that knowledge onto others. If he did, they would become obsessed and change outcomes and shit. It could get messy and archaic, so he kept his knowledge to himself, unless it slipped out, like it had now.

Like Kendrick knew, Fallon came… hard, all over his dick. Her walls tightened around him, and he looked down to see a creamy substance coating his dick. He licked his lips and pulled out of her before pushing his head between her legs and licking all that sweet frosting up.

"Ahh!" Fallon cried, her back lifting completely off the mattress. "Bae—"

"I know," Kendrick mumbled while keeping his lips on her swollen clit. She was on the brink of cumming again, and this time, he wanted to be there to catch all her sweet juices.

Fallon's legs shook violently as he repeatedly teased her clit, and within seconds, she was cumming again, this time squirting juices all over his thick beard. He moaned as he licked them up, and when her body went limp, he raised his head and licked his lips. "You good?"

"More than good," Fallon sighed, before sitting up and gently pushing Kendrick back.

He obliged, already knowing what was about to take place. When he was lying on his back, Fallon kissed the head of his dick, that was coated in her juices. His shit jumped like he had a mind of his own and was excited, and Fallon licked her lips in antici-pation. She loved giving head, and she was known to make big bad Kendrick tap out from her skills. The first time she gave him head, Kendrick sat in silence for an hour afterward, contemplating what the fuck had just happened.

Fallon's tongue flicked out and swiped at his shaft, causing Kendrick to shudder. When he felt her take him all into her mouth, he knew it was game over for him. She bobbed her head up and down at a steady pace, grasping his balls and allowing her spit to drip down onto them. Watching her full lips grip his dick was enough to make him spill his seed down her throat, but the way her mouth created a suction cup around his shit was his undoing.

"Fuck, bae," Kendrick growled. "I'm about to bust."

Fallon kept eye contact with him as she kept pace, staring at him sensually. She loved watching him cum. His love faces made her pussy drip, and just like that, she was ready for round two. Kendrick's dick swelled in her mouth, and Fallon pulled his dick out and jacked it slowly as his hot cum spilled onto her lips. She moaned as she licked the mess up and aimed for the rest to spill directly into her mouth.

"You're so fuckin' nasty," Kendrick groaned as he watched her taste him, his kids sitting neatly on her tongue and her lips. She was a pro like that.

When she swallowed, Kendrick pulled her up to him and kissed her full lips. He didn't give a fuck that his seed was just all over her. She was so damn irresistible, and he would kiss her whenever he felt the desire. He loved her without limitations, and she felt the same way about him.

Fallon pulled away from the kiss and rested her head on his chest, completely spent. The idea of round two was not completely out. She just needed a few minutes to regroup. What she didn't know was Kendrick knew round two was coming… as well as rounds three and four. He stretched, preparing for a long night, before wrapping his arms around her waist and resting his head on the top of hers.

Before Fallon could doze off, she had to ask something that had been on her mind since they got him.

"Will Papa be—"

"No," Kendrick replied, already knowing what she was going to ask.

Unfortunately, Papa would not be successful in turning the poor human that was downstairs, not realizing what their fate was. Fallon closed her eyes tightly, taking in a deep breath before releasing it slowly, letting go of the anxiety surrounding the situation. She had learned long ago not to take on the burdens of the gang because that shit would more than likely drive her insane… or kill her.

She nodded slowly against his chest and nestled into him, saying a silent prayer to whatever higher being would listen for the person downstairs that wouldn't make it to tomorrow.

KISSES across her face woke Fallon out of her sleep. She smiled with her eyes closed as she felt Kendrick kiss what seemed like each of her freckles.

"Good morning, Beauty," Kendrick mumbled against her bronzed skin.

Fallon's eyes fluttered as she focused her green eyes on him. She reached up and tugged on his beard, pulling him close to her so she could peck him on the lips. "Good morning, baby."

"How did you sleep?" he asked.

Fallon stretched and made the little screeching sound all women made when they stretched first thing in the morning. Kendrick waited patiently, and she finally settled down and responded, "Like shit, thanks to you."

Kendrick threw his head back and laughed, his gold fangs flashing in the morning sunlight that was filtering in through the blinds. "How you figure it's my fault?"

Fallon eyed him like he lost his damn mind. "Was it not you that kept waking me up for some pussy?"

Kendrick thought her fake attitude was cute. He knew they both knew he did her body right all night long, and she was more relaxed than she had been in a very long time. He could see it in her body language and the easy flow of her tone.

"If my memory serves me right," Kendrick replied cockily, because they both knew his memory did serve him right. Another perk to being a vampire. "You woke me up one of those times by sliding down on my dick. Right or wrong?"

Fallon smacked her lips together. "Whatever."

"Uh huh." Kendrick chuckled.

"What time is it?" Fallon asked, and Kendrick scrunched his faces up at the smell of her morning breath.

Fallon giggled. "Boy, bye. What time is it?" she asked again.

Kendrick leaned over and grabbed his phone from the nightstand. "Almost noon."

"Damn," Fallon replied. They normally didn't sleep that late, since Kendrick only needed five hours of sleep a day, tops. Vampires definitely slept. It was just a lot less. They could even go days without sleep if they wanted to. Fallon tried to keep up with their sleep schedule, but she had to remind herself that she was just a human amongst otherworldly creatures. She found out quickly she needed her eight hours every night. Five or less just wouldn't cut it. Still, they were normally up by nine at the latest. It was rare that they slept in, and that was how she knew they overexerted themselves the night before.

She nudged him, and he flipped over to his side so he was lying next to her.

"I'm going to freshen up," Fallon said, before getting out of bed and stretching one more time.

Kendrick laid there and admired her body. She was like a goddess in his eyes. He wanted to run his fingers through her tangled ginger hair, but he refrained. Instead, he watched as she walked into the bathroom and closed the door.

He looked down at his dick, which was hard as a brick once again. "Pipe down, lil' homie. Beauty needs some rest."

After his talk with his dick, he looked down at his phone that was still in his hand and checked his notifications. His jaw clenched when he saw a text from his mother.

Mother: *Son, how are you?*

He opted out of responding. He flopped onto his back and stared up at the ceiling, trying to remember the last time he saw his parents. He talked to them maybe once a year, but he hadn't seen them in a long ass time, and for good reason.

"Has to be about fifty years now," he mumbled to himself. Fifty years to a vampire was equivalent to a year or two to a vampire, but Kendrick knew his mother's text was because she was sick of him avoiding them.

"What has to be fifty years?"

Kendrick had been so deep in thought, he hadn't even heard Fallon come back into the room from the connecting bathroom. That was exactly what his parents did to him… they knocked him off his game.

"My mom just texted me," he replied. Fallon stiffened. She had only heard stories of the king and queen of The Guild, which was the court that ruled over all vampires. From what she knew… they were ruthless, but they loved their son, Kendrick. He loved them too, in his own way, but he did what he could to protect himself and those he loved from them.

"What did she want?" Fallon asked, trying to sound nonchalant. Something about his parents didn't sit right with her. Maybe it was the fact that they wanted Kendrick to take over The Guild, even though he wanted no parts, or maybe it was their abilities. His mother, Prima, could turn any creature's bones to dust with one simple touch. Of course, vampires could recover from that. After several days, their bones would regenerate, but it was debilitating enough for The Guild to move them to a cold climate or drive a stake through their heart to kill them for good. Word on the street was they had a freezer jail in the underground of their mansion in Jamaica, where they currently resided. They kept all their prisoners there because death was the easy way out. Being alive but frozen was a more suitable torture for anyone that spited them. Fallon shivered at the thought before her mind moved to Maximus, Kendrick's father. His ability was influence. He could make any living creature do whatever it was he wanted.

She knew if she ever found herself in their presence, she would do everything she could to get on their good side because there was no way she would ever want to be influenced into doing whatever Maximus wanted, and she damn sure didn't want her bones to turn to dust.

"She just asked how I was doing," he replied.

Fallon relaxed slightly as she went into the closet to get dressed.

"That was nice of her… right?" she called as she put on a pair of jeans followed by a fitted black hoodie that read *gang* across her breasts.

Before Kendrick could respond, the door to their

bedroom popped open, and Papa came in looking like shit. He was hungover, with tears streaking his face. His hoodie was wrinkled, and his messy black hair was all over his head. "He's dead!"

Hearing Papa's voice, Fallon put down the brush she was using to comb out her hair and pulled it up into a messy bun before stepping into the bedroom. She walked straight over to Papa and gathered him into her arms. He sagged into her and let out a sob. She had been here before. Many times. Papa was always a wreck the day after he tried mating with someone. Luckily, she knew just how to shift his mind from the despair he felt.

"Hey," Fallon whispered, nudging him away from her slightly while still holding onto him.

"Yeah?" Papa replied miserably, as he brushed his silky black hair out of his face and peered down at his friend while tears splashed onto their hoodies.

"It's five o'clock somewhere, right?" Fallon asked, peering into Papa's eyes with a grin on her face.

Papa sniffled, always the dramatic one, and said, "I knew I liked you."

Fallon giggled and looped her arm through his before turning to Kendrick. "You want breakfast, baby?"

Kendrick was too lost in his phone to pay attention to what Fallon or Papa were talking about.

Fallon's brows pulled together, and she spoke a little louder. "Bae?"

Kendrick's eyes snapped up to hers, and he could sense that Fallon and Papa were on the verge of getting daytime wasted and having one of their bonding days, as he liked to call it. He normally stayed away when those days came around because he wasn't really into sulking over Papa's love life. He loved that Fallon had enough patience to deal with that shit, though, because everyone else in TFG had grown sick of it long ago. Unfortunately, he sensed that their future course of action was going to change once he told them about the text that had just come through to his phone.

"Y'all are going to have to take a rain check on the drinking," Kendrick replied, hopping up from the bed, not caring that he was butt ass naked in front of Papa. He wasn't paying attention, anyway.

Papa stomped his foot and pouted before asking, "And why the fuck is that? You know drinking is exactly what I ne—"

"Cut it, Pablo," Kendrick snapped as he searched for the clothes he'd been wearing the day prior.

Papa and Fallon looked at Kendrick with worry on their faces now. Kendrick never called Papa by his real name. For him to do so, they knew something serious happened. Forgetting about his love life woes for a moment, Papa released Fallon and stepped toward Kendrick, who now had basketball shorts on and was walking into the closet to grab a shirt.

"What's wrong?"

Kendrick didn't respond verbally. Instead, he tossed his phone to Papa, who caught it effortlessly, despite the hangover which was making him a bit sluggish. Papa peered down at the phone, and just that quickly, he snapped into gear, looking up at Kendrick and asking, "What do you need me to do?"

"Get Fallon out of here. I take it back, y'all can drink. Just not here. Go day drink at a bar or some shit. I don't care, but don't bring her back here until I give the okay," Kendrick replied, pulling a shirt over his head.

Fallon looked between them and asked, "Does anyone want to tell the human what the fuck is going on?"

Kendrick's eyes landed on Fallon, and his eyes softened. "It's my mother… she was texting to let me know they would be in town soon. Since I didn't respond to her initial text fast enough, she let me know they would be here *today*."

Fallon's eyes ballooned, and she had a million questions racing through her mind. Unfortunately for her, she was unable to ask a single one because Papa was tugging on her arm and pulling her from the room with Kendrick right behind them.

They made it through the house with no sign of Axel or Scarlette. They were most likely still asleep, but Kendrick was going to wake them up as soon as he got Fallon and Papa safely out of the door.

Fallon cringed when she saw a dead white man on the living room floor, surrounded by empty tequila bottles, no doubt all drunken by Papa.

Kendrick saw her stiffen, and he pulled her from Papa's grasp and picked her up into his arms, palming the back of her head into his neck to obscure her view. "Sorry you had to see that."

Fallon didn't respond. She shuddered and closed her eyes tightly as Kendrick carried her to the door.

"Take my bike," Kendrick said, grabbing his keys and Fallon's leather jacket from the foyer and tossing them to Papa. "It's already out front."

The gang had too many cars to even count. Kendrick was a car junkie. He actually assisted Carl Benz with creating the first vehicle. His passion for cars ran deep, and he collected cars like a four-year-old collected rocks. Each of the gang had several bikes, too. The garage was underground and housed all their toys, but he didn't want to waste time on all that right now. His shit was parked out front and ready to fuckin' go, and that was what they needed at the moment.

He sat Fallon down on the bench that sat in the foyer and ran back upstairs to grab her black leather boots. Fallon only had time to blink once before he was back standing in front of her and lifting her foot so he could put her shoes on.

"I got it," she said, grasping the boot and stuffing her foot inside.

As soon as she put the other one on, he lifted her up into his arms and kissed her on the cheek. "I'll call you as soon as I can, okay?"

Fallon didn't like how fast everything was happening, and she didn't like the vibes she was getting, but she trusted Kendrick enough to shove that worry away and whisper, "Okay."

He placed her on her feet, and Papa grabbed her hand before ushering them to the door. When he opened it, however, his brisk pace halted, causing Fallon to run right into his back.

"Ouch!" she grumbled before pushing at Papa's back. He didn't move, and Kendrick was at her side in a flash, holding her by the waist protectively as he looked into the eyes of his parents.

EACH OF KENDRICK'S parents wore sinister grins they tried to cover up as being friendly.

"Well, well, well, where are you off to in such a hurry, son?" Prima berated as she stepped inside the house as if someone had invited her, Maximus hot on his wife's heels.

"And you have a guest. How thoughtful of you to have breakfast waiting," Maximus said as he flashed his fangs, looking at Fallon hungrily. He had caramel colored skin with coal-black eyes, much like his son. His bald head and long beard gave him a distinguished look, but Fallon knew that air of wisdom about him was more because he was a thousand years old and not because of his beard or hair.

Kendrick stepped in front of her, and Prima's brows rose before she looked at her husband. "Darling, I don't think that's breakfast."

Maximus had already come to that same conclusion. "I believe you're right, sweetheart. Kendrick, who do we have here?"

Kendrick's jaw clenched so hard, it surprised him he didn't break a tooth… or several. He hated that he wasn't in tune with his parents like he once was. If he had been, he would have been able to sense their arrival. The only thing keeping him calm at the moment was that he didn't foresee any immediate danger toward Fallon or himself. He was in tune with Fallon in a way he wasn't with anyone else, so much like he could sense harm coming his way, he could sense that for Fallon, too.

Fallon noticed Kendrick wasn't going to respond to his parents, and they looked like they weren't the type of vampire that practiced patience, so she took in a deep breath and stepped forward. Or tried to, at least. Kendrick moved slightly to block her from fully stepping around him, and she huffed in response before looking at Maximus and saying, "I'm Fallon Bordeaux."

Prima's eyebrow rose slightly, and Maximus mimicked his son by clenching his jaw. They stared at Fallon for several long moments before Prima finally spoke up. "Bordeaux, huh? Were you born and raised here in New Orleans?"

Fallon opened her mouth to respond, but was cut

off by Kendrick. "She was just leaving. Her and Papa had plans for the day."

"Nonsense," Prima said with the wave of her hand, her long, elegant fingers giving a quick flick. "This young woman is obviously important to you. She will stay for breakfast so we can get to know her. She may be the answer to the reasoning for our visit."

"We didn't make breakfast," Kendrick said through clenched teeth.

The tension in the room was thick, and it was making Fallon extremely uncomfortable and nervous. Once again, she tried to step around Kendrick, but gave up when he wouldn't budge. She sighed heavily and said meekly, "I can make breakfast."

Kendrick stole a quick glace at her, and he wanted to be upset that he extended that offer, but he knew that was just who Fallon was. She didn't thrive in tension. It was a trigger for her because when they met; it caused a lot of tension in the home she grew up in with her grandmother, to the point that they didn't even speak anymore. Since then, she always tried to play the peacemaker. That wasn't to get anything confused, though. If conflict was what mothafuckas around her were dead set on having, she was with the shits, but if it could be avoided, she would do everything she could to take that route.

"Wonderful," Prima chirped before looking at her son, who looked so much like her. Kendrick had his father's eyes, but his mother's face, just with facial hair. Her skin was dark, her thick brows were tweezed and waxed perfectly, and her amber-colored eyes were slanted and piercing. She was tall for a woman, even taller than Fallon, who wasn't short herself, and Prima was slender with the body of a ballerina. Prima reached out and patted her son's cheek. "You look good, son. It's been entirely too long." She looked at Papa and said, "Do show me around, Papa. I haven't had the pleasure of being invited to this dwelling."

Papa looked at Kendrick, who gave a slight nod. Papa placed a stiff smile on his face and said, "Right this way. We can start on this floor and work our way up."

Prima smiled at him and looped her arm through her husband's. "Come, Maximus. Let's give them time to prepare our food."

Kendrick watched as they disappeared into the study that was right off the foyer before he picked Fallon up and dashed up the stairs. Fallon was dizzy with how fast they moved. When Kendrick put her down, they were in Scarlett's room.

"Scar! Wake up," Kenderick said with plenty of bass in his voice.

Scarlette's room was was decorated in deep red and black. The curtains were closed and blackout, blanketing everything in complete darkness. Fallon couldn't see shit, but she knew the two vamps in the room could see everything as if it were daylight. She stood in complete stillness, grabbing onto Kendrick's hand for some sense of balance.

A few seconds later, sunlight engulfed the room, and Scarlette was standing at the window looking like she just rose from the dead. Her long black hair was matted to the side of her head, sticking to her face. Her face was bare of any makeup, and her eyes pierced Kendrick's as one of her already highly arched brows rose.

"Whats wrong?" she asked, her voice hoarse from a long night of partying.

"My parents are here," Kendrick replied, walking to her closet and pulling a pair of leggings and an oversized t-shirt out of one of her drawers.

When he came back into the room, Scarlette was still standing in the same place, staring at Fallon, and then back at Kendrick. "Here as in they are in town?"

"Here as in, they are somewhere in this house getting the grand tour from Papa."

Scarlette's eyes widened, and Kendrick tossed the clothes he picked out for her in her direction. She caught them and pulled the leggings on quickly. She was about to pull off her nightshirt, but Kendrick didn't stay around to watch her getting dressed. He turned on his heels and called over his shoulder, "Help Fallon cook breakfast. I'm going to wake Axel."

Even though he wasn't looking, Scarlette nodded her head before pulling her nightshirt off just as Kendrick closed the door. Fallon watched as Scarlette pulled the fresh t-shirt Kendrick gave her over her head. One thing about vampires was they were not shy at all. They would strip in front of anyone and acted as if they were merely putting on a pair of shoes.

Scarlette's B cup breasts heaved as she sighed heavily and pulled her shirt over her head before dashing to the bathroom to comb through her hair. Fallon followed behind her and asked, "Is this bad?"

Scarlette stopped brushing for a second and looked at Fallon in the mirror. "Prima and Maximus haven't reigned as king and queen for almost a thousand years by being pleasant."

Fallon nodded curtly. "Why do you think they're here?"

"There's no telling. It's been years since I last saw them. I know Kendrick has seen them a few times since I have, but normally, their visits are planned and more of a formality. This feels different. They've never just popped up on him before." Scarlette finished brushing her hair before spinning on her heels and grasping Fallon's hand, not giving her a chance to respond.

The two hurried out of the room and down the long, dimly lit hallway, Fallon practically sprinting to keep up with Scarlette. When they made it to the large industrial kitchen, Scarlette let go of Fallon's hand and immediately went to work grabbing stuff out of the refrigerator and setting them on the large black and grey island in the middle of the room.

"Can you scramble some eggs while I mix up this pancake batter?" Scarlette asked as she took an onion and pepper out of the refrigerator and tossed them to Fallon, who caught the onion, but the pepper smacked her on the shoulder and hit the ground before rolling several feet away. Scarlette stopped rummaging around in the refrigerator and popped her head out before saying, "Sorry, Fal. Sometimes I forget you aren't a vamp."

"Yeah," Fallon mumbled, as she bent to pick up the pepper before placing the vegetables on the island and walking over to the cupboard that held the cutting boards.

As Fallon chopped the onions and peppers for the eggs, she got lost in her thoughts. Shit was happening fast today, and she wasn't sure what to make of it. She wished she could be up under Kendrick at that moment, and not stuck making breakfast, but she had offered, and she knew better than to go back on that offer. Still, she wished like hell she understood the reason for the king and queen's impromptu visit so she could be better prepared.

When the vegetables were chopped and sauteing in the pan on the stove, Fallon got to work on cracking eggs into a big bowl while Scarlette threw bacon, sausage, and biscuits in the oven before she prepared the griddle for the pancakes. Scarlette loved cooking. It was something she and Fallon bonded over. Scarlette had been cooking for centuries, and Fallon picked up her love for cooking from her grandmother. Thoughts of her made Fallon uneasy, and Maximus and Prima visiting was enough unease for the day, so she pushed those thoughts to the side and focused on the task at hand.

The two best friends worked in silence, and it wasn't long before Kendrick and Axel came into the kitchen, looking alert and rigid. Fallon stepped away from the stove where the eggs were cooking and walked directly into Kendrick's arms. She looked up at him. "You good?"

He nodded stiffly before asking, "How's the food coming along?"

Fallon shrugged and looked guiltily at Scarlette. "The eggs are almost done. I haven't been much help, Scar, sorry."

"It's fine," Scarlette chirped, trying to keep up a positive energy. "I knew that brilliant mind of yours would be busy thinking. Breakfast is almost finished."

Fallon loved Scarlette more than she ever had at that moment. She was the one that offered Prima and Maximus breakfast, yet she was barely able to deliver on that offer because she was too busy overthinking shit. Scarlette had come through for her in a major way, and Fallon realized Kendrick most likely foresaw that she would need help, which was why he woke Scarlette up in the first place. Typically, cooking for the gang was no issue for Fallon to handle on her own. Cooking was therapeutic to her. It reminded her so much of chemistry, which was where she really thrived. Mixing chemicals and components to create something was fascinating to her.

"Good, I'm starving," Prima said from behind them. Fallon stiffened, but she noticed everyone else in the room went on about their business. Of course they had. They would have heard the three vampires sneaking up behind them. Papa strolled into the kitchen with a tight smile on his face before grabbing a hot biscuit from the counter and stuffing it into his mouth. Nobody stopped him because they all knew his ass needed the carbs to soak up the liquor he consumed early into the morning.

"Any chance there's some fresh blood around here? I'd hate to feast off the human in the other room. There's nothing worse than cold blood," Maximus asked, his eyes landing on Fallon with a glint.

Kendrick held her tighter by the waist and said, "If you wanted blood, you should have brought your own. We don't keep humans around to feed on whenever we feel like it."

"Why ever not?" Prima asked, genuinely appalled.

"You used to be so much more fun, son. What happened?" Maximus followed up behind his wife.

Kendrick caressed Fallon's side. It was an involuntary answer. The gesture was subtle, but Prima and Maximus noticed. A sly grin graced Prima's face as she glanced at her husband and then back at Kendrick. "How about we eat? We can worry about the blood later."

It was more of a demand than a question, so without any more words being exchanged, each member of TFG grabbed a dish and walked into the dining room following the king and queen.

THE TENSION in the room could be cut with a fang. Fallon kept a cool demeanor, but she was nervous as hell, and she knew Kendrick could tell. Most likely, if he could tell, so could everyone else at the table, which was just fucking great. The last thing she needed was to appear weak in front of this crowd.

It was silent as they ate, Prima and Maximus at either end of the table, while Kendrick sat next to his father. Fallon sat in between Kendrick and Prima while Papa, Axel, and Scarlette sat across from her. Utensils clanked against plates while everyone ate aside from Kendrick. Fallon had to admit she was having a hard time finding her appetite, but again, she didn't want to be rude, so she took the smallest amount possible without being obvious and forced it down her throat.

She glanced at Kendrick, and she could instantly feel his unease. She was always hypersensitive to other's feelings, and the energy Kendrick was putting into the atmosphere was palpable to her. Briefly, she wondered if he needed human blood. It had been a few days since he had taken any from her, and she knew she was the only human he would drink from. Vampires needed human blood a few times a week to sustain their abilities. Not only that, when they didn't have human blood, they got moody first and then severe illness followed. Papa refused human blood for a month one time after a particularly hard time after trying to turn a mate. Fallon had never seen a more pathetic sight. The migraines they experienced were debilitating and they couldn't keep food down. Chills would run through their body, mimicking how their bodies shut down when they were in the cold. If they went long enough without human blood, their limbs would freeze up. That normally took three months. Much like the cold wouldn't kill them, not consuming human blood wouldn't, either, but it was extremely painful and something every sane vampire avoided.

She reached under the table and grasped his hand. After giving it a squeeze, she side eyed him again and saw him relax, but only slightly.

To ease the tension, Fallon decided to try her

hand at conversation. "How long are you in town for, Mr. and Mrs. Danger?"

Prima stopped eating the sausage she had been gnawing on and peered down her slender nose at Fallon, who was sitting right next to her. After several long seconds, Prima said, "I'm sorry, dear. What was your name again?"

Fallon opened her mouth to respond, but Kendrick interrupted her. "Ma, come on, now. You know her name."

"It's okay, baby," Fallon said, squeezing Kendrick's hand once again before looking back at Prima. "Fallon."

"Bordeaux was the last name, right?" she asked casually as she took a sip of her orange juice.

"Yes, ma'am," Fallon replied.

"Who are your people?" Prima asked after a few moments of silence while everyone resumed eating.

"Why are you here?" Kendrick asked, sick of all the questions. He was uneasy because he didn't know what the fuck his parents were up to, but he didn't trust them. He knew them well enough to know they had an ulterior motive for being there. He was never that important to his parents for them to just pop up on him unless there was a reason.

"Apologize," Maximus demanded after dropping his fork on his plate.

"No disrespect, father, but I'm not with this popping up shit. I just want to know why the hell y'all are here."

Maximus stared his son down for several long seconds before Kendrick's face softened and he looked at his mother lovingly. "Sorry, Mama."

He shook his head vigorously before glaring back at his father. "Cut that shit out. I told you about doing that shit to me."

Fallon's eyes grew wide when she realized what had just happened. Maximus made Kendrick apologize to his mother against his will. She closed her eyes for a moment and took in a deep breath, trying to calm her nerves, before she tuned back into the conversation.

"What good is having an ability if I can't use it?" Maximus asked arrogantly, almost as if he was daring his son to argue.

Kendrick's jaw flexed as he glared at his father. Fallon shivered involuntarily. She wasn't really afraid, because not much scared her, but she did feel a little like a sheep amongst wolves. She knew she had no power within this environment, but one thing about Fallon, she didn't allow fear to control her, so she kept her features under control and took subtle deep breaths to calm her heart, knowing the vampires in the room could hear the shit as if Nick

Cannon was in the room practicing for his role on *Drumline.*

"Now, now, Max. It's quite alright," Prima intervened, and something told Fallon that it in fact was not alright. She could tell the queen wasn't used to being interrupted or having her questions ignored, but it was obvious she wanted something, so she was playing shit cool. Prima turned to Kendrick and said, "To answer your question, dear, we have come to see how you're progressing on finding a romantic mate. Axel, of course, does not count. Unless you're now in a relationship with him. It would be unconventional to have two kings, but I supposed we coul—"

"No, ma'am. We are not in a relationship," Axel interrupted, his face stone cold as he gazed at the queen. Fallon wanted to laugh at how pissed Axel looked at the thought of being romantically mated to Kendrick, but she was too caught up in confusion to do so. She glanced at Kendrick with her brows raised slightly before she rearranged her features and patiently waited for Kendrick's response. She had no idea his parents were waiting for him to mate to someone.

"You know my stance on finding a mate," Kendrick said through clenched fangs.

"And you know how we feel about it," Prima quipped before taking a bite of her eggs.

"Son, you know you need to find a mate in order to take over The Guild," Maximus cut in, looking at Kendrick with a hardened glare.

Fallon's eyes grew wide, and this time, she didn't mask her surprise. She knew Kendrick's parents wanted him to take over The Guild, but she didn't know they predicated it on him having a mate. She was a bit hurt by this revelation. If Kendrick's parents had an expectation of him to mate to someone in order to take over their family empire, why wouldn't that be something Kendrick would tell her? Then a more painful thought came to her. What if he was hoping his parents wouldn't come back around and bug him about this situation until after her lifetime? Fallon mimicked her man and clenched her jaw tightly to keep from addressing this shit in front of everyone.

"I need more time. I'm working on it," Kendrick replied, keeping his eyes on his parents and ignoring Fallon's heated glare.

Prima's red painted lips curved into a smile. "Wonderful." Her eyes flicked over to Fallon before she asked, "And how does Ms. Bordeaux fit into all of this?"

Fallon crossed her arms over her chest and looked at Kendrick, waiting for his answer. Kendrick could feel the heat coming off her in waves. Papa cleared his throat while Axel stopped eating completely. Scarlette looked at Fallon, trying to catch her eye so she could reassure her best friend, but Fallon was entirely too focused on the man she loved. The man who just admitted that he had been working on finding a mate behind her back.

When it became clear that Kendrick was not going to respond, Prima tried a different approach. "How long have you two been seeing each other?"

"Who said we were seeing each other?" Kendrick asked.

"Kendrick," Fallon snapped, now seething at his blatant disrespect for her. She stared at him for a few moments before scoffing and turning to Prima. "Four years."

"Four years?" the queen asked. "That's a long time for a human." She turned to Kendrick. "Are you planning to turn Ms. Bordeaux so you can take over The Guild?"

"I don't want to take over The Guild, you know that," Kendrick replied. He was heated that his parents had put him in this situation. He knew he needed to get Fallon alone so he could explain some things to her. He never wanted to put pressure on her about turning, because turning her was never something he wanted to do. He promised himself Axel was the last person he turned, and he had kept that promise for centuries. Even in the name of love, he wasn't willing to go back on that promise because he knew he wouldn't be able to live with the guilt of cutting Fallon's life short if she died instead of turning into a vampire.

"Then why are you working on turning a mate?" Maximus asked coolly.

Kendrick looked at his father. He knew Maximus was trying to catch him in a lie. Kendrick knew they both knew he hadn't been looking for a mate, even though Fallon probably thought otherwise based on his previous statement. He also knew his father had the power to make Kendrick tell the truth. He couldn't allow that, either, so he knew he had to throw his parents off. Without thinking about it thoroughly, he blurted out, "Fallon and I agreed I would turn her after our wedding."

The room went silent as Fallon looked at Kendrick with wide eyes, anger simmering just below the surface.

SHE FIXED her face quickly before anyone could catch a glimpse of her. By the time the king and queen, along with everyone else, looked at her, she arranged her face back into the passive mask of subtle nervousness, which also wasn't a front. She was nervous as hell and had no idea what the fuck was going on. For one, she didn't remember Kendrick ever getting down on one knee. For two, she damn sure never agreed to be bitten by him on their damn honeymoon.

"Wedding?" Prima asked, her dark eyes instantly lighting up at the thought of such an event. "Oh, Kendrick, why didn't you tell us? Where is the ring?"

Fallon was sure Prima hadn't known about the wedding because the supposed bride herself didn't even know about the shit, but because she felt so out of place, and she wasn't sure what the fuck was even going on, she stayed quiet and played with the food on the plate in front of her while the vampires talked about her life as if she wasn't even sitting there. Prima glanced once again at Fallon's ring finger, and Fallon dropped her hands into her lap and out of view.

"I wanted the shit to be private, that's why. I know how carried away you can get. Fallon and I want something intimate. The ring is getting sized," Kendrick replied stiffly, lying through his fangs.

Prima waved her hand in a dismissive manner. "Nonsense."

"Ma—"

Kendrick was interrupted by his father, who said, "You already lost her, son. You know she loves planning events."

Maximus chuckled as Prima ticked off things she had to do on her fingers while she talked out loud to herself. Fallon watched them in utter confusion because, at that moment, the king and queen didn't look like original vampires who were just asking about human blood to go along with their breakfast. Instead, they looked like genuine parents who were excited about their son's upcoming nuptials.

Prima finally fixed her eyes on Scarlette and asked, "Are you a bridesmaid?"

"Maid of honor, actually," Scarlette replied with a

tight smile, and Fallon glared at her with confusion written all over her face.

Scarlette subtly shrugged her shoulders while Prima clapped her hands excitedly. "Wonderful." She turned to Fallon finally and asked, "And will there be any more in your part of the wedding party?"

"No, mother," Kendrick intervened before Fallon could respond. "Just Scarlette."

"Hmm… I like bigger wedding parties, but I can understand the lack of family or friends," Prima rambled. Fallon opened her mouth to correct Prima, but then she closed her mouth because she realized the woman wasn't entirely wrong. The only friends she had were sitting in this room, and her grandmother wanted nothing to do with her. She had nobody else, so even if she was getting married, Scarlette would be the only one standing by her side. That thought saddened her slightly, but Prima's voice caused her to push those thoughts to the side for the time being. "And who is the groomsman? Papa? Axel?"

Kendrick's jaw twitched before he said, "Axel."

"And I'm the flower girl," Papa chimed in, happy to play along with whatever bullshit Kendrick was getting them into.

Prima barked out a laugh that startled Fallon. She jumped slightly, and Kendrick automatically reached out his free hand, since she had dropped it earlier, and touched her knee to comfort her, but Fallon pulled away from him.

"The flower girl," Prima said with laughter still in her voice. "It certainly isn't traditional, but I suppose I can allow that—"

"Allow it?" Kendrick asked incredulously. "You have no say—"

"A wedding within the royal family? I'd say I have all the say," Prima snapped, returning to her former cold self. Kendrick stared her down, but she barely seemed to notice. "We can plan a turning ceremony directly after the wedding. It'll be perfect. You'll be a queen, darling."

Prima's piercing eyes drilled holes into Fallon's as the only human in the room desperately tried to keep her head from spinning. Shit was happening entirely too fast. *Queen?* She didn't want to be a queen or a vampire.

"We aren't going to turn her right away, Mother. We are going to wait for a few years—"

"No. You will turn her right away. Your father and I are ready to retire. Maybe in a few centuries we will be willing to take over The Guild again... or maybe you will have children of your own to do so, but we came here to let you know by the end of the year you needed to find a mate and begin your reign.

If you are unable to find a mate by the end of the year, you will still step in as the head of The Guild while your father and I take more of a backseat. Once you find your mate, we will step down completely. We have been the head of The Guild since we turned. We are tired."

She stretched out the last few words to drive home her point, but Kendrick wasn't trying to hear any of that. "Why not hand it over to one of your trusted members?"

"Are you insane?" Maximus spoke up. "The Guild is to stay within our family. No excuses, and that is final."

"You can't just force this on me," Kendrick rebutted.

Maximus didn't respond. He simply stared at his son menacingly, driving his point home. Everyone understood what Maximus didn't even have to say. He could, in fact, compel his son to take over The Guild. All he would have to do was use his ability.

Kendrick gritted his teeth. Resigned, he said, "We weren't planning on getting married for a few years—"

"You'll get married in exactly one month. That's enough time to plan an extravagant wedding and get your affairs in order," Prima replied, her eyes landing on Fallon by the end of her declaration.

Fallon swallowed the lump in her throat and stood to her feet abruptly. "I'm not feeling so well, so I'm going to excuse myself. It was nice meeting you, Mr. and Mrs. Danger."

Without waiting for a response, Fallon turned on her heels and made a beeline out of the dining room and up the stairs, straight toward her and Kendrick's room. Once she was behind closed doors, she immediately paced the length of the room as she tried sorting out the last hour and a half. She had met the vampire king and queen, learned that Kendrick needed to be mated and had possibly been searching for a mate behind her back, and was now supposedly getting married within the next month. The kicker was the part about her being turned into a vampire against her will. Truthfully, Fallon valued her life. She didn't want to turn because she was afraid of dying. That was one thing that scared her. Death was never appealing to her, aside from watching it happen in movies. What if she and Kendrick weren't true mates? It was a thought that always plagued her.

Several long minutes later, after Fallon damn near walked a hole through the floor from all her pacing, Kendrick walked into the room and closed the door behind him. "Baby—"

"What the fuck did you get me into, Kendrick?"

Fallon snapped, cutting him off. "Have you really been trying to find your mate while stringing me along?"

Depending on his response, Fallon was ready to fuck him up. Vampire or not… she was about to take it there and put some work in on his ass, and they both knew he would have no choice but to let her exhaust all her anger. The love they shared… Kendrick knew that would be the ultimate betrayal, so he quickly did his best to reassure her. He walked over to her and gathered her into his arms. She struggled against him, but stopped when she realized he wasn't going to let her go.

"Baby… no. I haven't. I said that to try to appease them. I had no idea the shit was going to take such a turn," he replied.

She was relieved to hear that, at least. She wasn't sure how she would have handled him trying to be mated to someone else but her. Then she wondered if she was being selfish. Kendrick deserved an eternity of love. She wasn't willing to take that chance with him, so why shouldn't he look for that in someone else? That only made her sad, then angry again because of the audacity of him to live and learn to love after her. She knew she wasn't being rational, but she couldn't help it. Within the last hour and a half, she felt as though her life had been snatched from her.

"And why the fuck not?" Fallon asked, as she looked up at him. "You know everything else."

"You know my ability doesn't work like that, baby. I tried tapping in to see what the outcome of all this shit would be, but its murky. It's like there's an outside factor that hasn't been decided on yet," Kendrick replied, doing his best to explain it to her.

"An outside factor like what, Kendrick?"

He shrugged his shoulders before rubbing his hands up and down the length of her back. "I don't know, baby, but I promise to do everything in my power to put this shit off as long as possible. That was why I even mentioned a wedding. If I hadn't, they would have made me bite you right there at the table. If nothing else, Fallon, you have the right to walk away completely from this entire ordeal. I know you don't want to be a vampire—"

"I don't want to die," Fallon whispered. "It was never about being a vampire. I don't want to die, Kendrick. I don't want you to live with the guilt of killing me."

"I don't want that, either," he replied seriously.

Fallon stood there for a moment, deep in thought, before asking, "Why have you never been able to see if you could turn me or not?"

"My ability is the most finicky out of my family's, and the shit has always pissed me off, on gang. I've told you before that a decision has to be made before I can potentially see the future."

"Right," Fallon said slowly.

"We have never made a decision to turn you, Beauty. Because of that, I can't see if it would work or not. Even if we did make a decision, it's not one hundred percent that I'll see the outcome."

"But there's a better chance because you're so in tune with me, right?" Fallon asked.

"Right," Kendrick replied.

Fallon sighed and stepped out of his embrace. Kendrick allowed her a little space, but he still grasped her hand so she couldn't get too far away.

"Then we need to make a decision," Fallon whispered.

"I can't ask you to do that. Not because of my parents. They don't get to come in here and—"

"Do you really want to marry me?" Fallon asked, feeling extremely vulnerable. They had never talked about marriage, but they had talked about spending a lifetime together. Fallon's lifetime, that was. Marriage was something neither of them brought up because it was already understood that they would be together for as long as the universe allowed. Now that it was on the table, Fallon wanted to know his thoughts on it.

Kendrick's face softened, and for a moment, all his worries melted away as he stared at the only woman he had ever truly loved. "More than anything."

Fallon searched his eyes, and all she saw was the truth, which reassured her to share this next bit of information. "Then I may have a solution."

THAT SOLUTION WAS in the form of a cure for vampire venom. Fallon had been spending the last few years experimenting with Kendrick's venom and trying to come up with the cure to surviving a vampire bite so she could properly turn. Vampires could bite humans, and they would dispense a small portion of their venom into the human's bloodstream to give off a euphoric feeling and numb the pain. They injected more venom once they completely drained the body of blood. That full dose of venom was either deadly or would turn a human. She wasn't even sure it was possible to cure it, which was why she had kept her experiments to herself, but when Kendrick's parents showed up a couple of weeks ago, turning their lives upside down, she figured that was the perfect time to let her man in on her little secret.

That little secret had been running her life for the past couple of weeks. She woke up and went straight to school to work on the cure. In between classes, she was in the lab. Kendrick would pick her up at ten at night when campus closed, even on her days off from classes and weekends. She spent all her time trying to perfect the cure, and the day finally came where she thought she got it right.

Fallon removed her goggles and smiled widely at the vial in her hand that contained a bright blue concoction before pulling her phone out to call Kendrick.

He answered after only a couple of seconds. "Beauty, I don't care about that cure tonight. I'll be there in a few minutes, and that's final."

Fallon giggled. She knew Kendrick was fed up with her, but she was glad she actually had some good news for him that day. "I was just calling to let you know I'm ready. I think I actually had a breakthrough."

The line was silent for a moment before Kendrick said, "Word?"

His tone was not lost on Fallon. He sounded like he was forcing his voice to sound jovial.

"What's wrong?" she asked.

"Nothing, bae," Kendrick said with a sigh. "You made a cure, huh?"

"Yup! I really think I did it, baby. I told you all these long hours would pay off," Fallon bragged, as she cradled her phone to her ear with her shoulder and cleaned up her workstation. Thankfully, nobody was in the lab with her that day, and why would they be? It was a Saturday. Even the nerdiest of nerds wasn't in the labs on Saturdays, which worked out just fine for her. She didn't like being bothered when she was working, especially on something as important as the cure for a vampire bite. She already had peers and professors questioning her about what she had been doing over the past few weeks, but she had played it off so far.

"Yeah, you did…" he hesitated before he said, "I ain't gon' lie, not being able to read the future surrounding this situation has been fuckin' wit' me, but I'm proud of you for working so hard to find that cure. I can't believe this is something you been working on for the past few years. You're smart as fuck, Beauty," Kendrick said.

Fallon's cheeks warmed. Shit had been stressful for them. There hadn't been too many conversations surrounding the future because shit was so in the air, but they tried to stay positive. Fallon didn't tell Kendrick that she hadn't been sleeping because she had become obsessed with death and what it would feel like. She was terrified she wouldn't survive to see the end of the year. Her mind kept wandering to her grandmother, and she had been debating on if she should reach out to her in order to make amends… just in case.

Kendrick, on the other hand, had been slowly losing his mind over the entire situation. He talked to his parents damn near every day and had tried tirelessly to push this wedding and biting ceremony back, but they wouldn't budge. Bottom line was they were tired of running The Guild, and they were ready for him to step up. Desperately, Kendrick even asked them if Fallon could be the queen as a human, and they laughed in his face at that.

They compelled some humans that lived not even a mile away from The Lair to allow them to live in their home until the wedding was over and they could return to Jamaica. It was a win-win for them because the humans were compelled to stick around and be human blood bags to the two vampires. Luckily, vampire venom had a property in it that caused humans to forget being bitten as soon as it was over. It was a contingency to make sure humans never found out about them. Once the king and queen left, the humans they were infringing on would go on about their lives as if nothing happened.

"Thanks, baby," Fallon replied, as she wiped down her workstation before putting the vial with the cure in her backpack. "I'm ready. I'll be out front when you get here."

"Bet," Kendrick replied. "I'm pulling up in a few."

They disconnected the call, and Fallon shut off the lights in the lab and exited the classroom. She took her time making her way through the campus as she took in the scenery. She was glad there were barely any students around the classrooms. They were all in their dorms or off campus, so she didn't have to worry about Kendrick's little fan club that day.

The campus truly was beautiful, and she found herself basking in the smallest things lately. Tears hadn't come to her. Fallon wasn't really a crier. Not that she never cried, she just took things as they came and dealt with them as best as she could. As the time grew closer, she would most likely become more nervous, and there probably would be some tears, but focusing on finding a cure helped to block everything else out for the time being.

By the time she got to the spot Kendrick always picked her up, he was there, waiting for her beside his black Ducati bike. He was dressed in all black, and his full beard seemed to glisten in the sun along with his smooth dark skin. Fallon almost tripped over her own feet as she hurried into his arms. When he closed his arms around her, she breathed him in.

He smelled so damn good… like mahogany and pine needles.

"Hey, Beauty," Kendrick murmured into her ginger hair, hugging her tighter than normal.

"Baby," Fallon replied as a way of greeting.

They stood in the embrace for several long moments before Fallon pulled away slightly and said, "Let's get out of here. I've been spending enough time here lately."

"Say that shit again," Kendrick mumbled, and Fallon shook her head with a giggle.

Kendrick handed her a black helmet with red letters on the back that read *GANG*. He put his matching one on his head before mounting the bike. Fallon made sure her backpack was snug on her shoulders before putting her helmet on and climbing on behind him.

Kendrick turned the bike on and skirted out of the parking lot while Fallon rested against his back with her eyes closed, soaking in the nice breeze and the strong muscles in Kendrick's back as they flexed with every movement.

The forty-five-minute ride didn't seem to take long before they were pulling up to The Lair. When the bike stopped in front, Fallon hopped off and waited patiently for Kendrick to join her. When he did, he grabbed her in his arms again and said, "I love you."

The way he said it made a lump form in Fallon's throat. She looked up at him and blinked back tears before saying, "I love you, too."

"I know I got you in this situation, but I want you to know I love you enough to give you an out. I don't want to live without you, but if I have to, I want it to be because you are choosing to live your life how you see fit instead of you dying by my fangs."

Fallon shook her head sharply with her brows furrowed. "Baby, no… that isn't what I want. That's the last thing I want. I'm scared… I won't lie—"

"I know. You haven't been sleeping. I've noticed the shift in you, Beauty. I just didn't want to feed into it. That's why I'm giving you another chance to get out—"

"I don't want that," Fallon said harshly. "Stop saying that. A life without you isn't a life at all. This cure is going to work. I have to believe that because I'm not going anywhere. I want to live, and whatever we have to do to ensure that, we will. End of story."

Kendrick stared down at her for a few more moments. He was conflicted, and his cold heart ached, but he pushed past all that before asking, "You sure?"

Fallon didn't hesitate. "Positive."

Kendrick nodded his head and took her by the hand, leading her up the stairs and to the front door. He opened it for her and stepped aside. Fallon was too busy giving him a reassuring smile, worried that he didn't believe that she wanted to stay with him, that she didn't realize the foyer was decorated with flowers, and the entire gang was there with smiling faces, fangs showing and all.

"Surprise!" they yelled, startling Fallon. She grasped her chest before taking a step back, damn near tripping over Kendrick, who she noticed was on one knee behind her once she got her footing.

This time, she didn't stop the tears from falling from her eyes as she straightened up with his help before fully facing him with a hand covering her mouth as she stared down at the teardrop shaped ruby ring that sat in a black velvet box in Kendrick's hands.

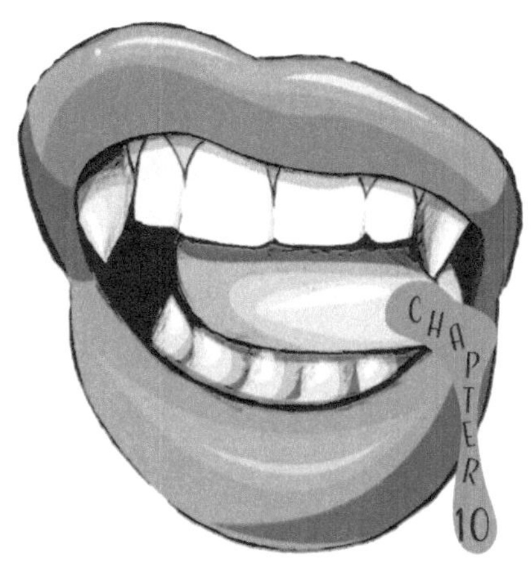

"I'VE WANTED to marry you since the moment I laid eyes on you, Fallon," Kendrick said as he looked up at the love of his life. She was so beautiful to him, and he had everything about her embedded into his brain, down to every last one of her freckles. The way he loved this woman was almost unhealthy. He always assumed there would be a time when he wouldn't be able to see her beautiful smile anymore, and because of that, he obsessed over her while he had her. The decision to marry her was an easy one, and as soon as she confirmed she wasn't leaving him only moments ago, he saw what her answer would be, which gave him all the confidence in the world to follow through with this proposal.

Tears cascaded down Fallon's cheeks while she gazed down at Kendrick. Her heart beat wildly. Of course, they were getting married. They were being forced to do so. She never once took the time to slow down and realize that this was real. She would be devoting her life, hopefully an eternity, to this man. Why shouldn't they turn this nightmare into a fairytale? At that moment, Fallon was grateful to Kendrick for having the foresight to do so. Then again, of course, he did.

"I bought this ring a few years ago, but I never knew if marriage was in the cards for us. I know the way this all came about is unconventional, but through all the bullshit, I can't lie and say I'm not excited about being your husband, whether that's for a lifetime or an eternity, so I'm asking—"

"Yes!" Fallon shouted, the word bubbling up so fast from deep within her that she wasn't able to keep it in.

There was a chorus of laughter behind them as Kendrick's eyes crinkled from the smile that spread across his face. "Damn, I couldn't even get the rest of my speech out?"

"Boy, fuck that rehearsed speech! The answer is yes!" Fallon screeched happily while she held her left hand out so he could put the ring on her finger.

"That's my girl," Scarlette called from behind them, and there was more laughter from the men.

Kendrick shook his head playfully before standing up and placing the ring on Fallon's ring finger. She admired it with fresh tears in her eyes before tilting her head up and grabbing Kendrick's face in both her hands. "Thank you, baby."

"I would do anything for you, Beauty. No matter what happens, I will keep you alive. You have my word," Kendrick said, his lips brushing against hers.

Fallon kissed him, pulling him in closer so he could feel her energy at capacity. She wanted him to really understand what he meant to her and what this moment meant to her.

When they broke apart, the rest of the gang cheered their congratulations before Scarlette and Papa were at Fallon's side. "Sorry to take you away from your mans, but we have work to do."

"Work to do? What do you mea—"

Fallon couldn't get her question out fully before the two vamps whisked her off her feet and out of the foyer. Seconds later, they were in Scarlette's room, and Fallon was dizzy from the quick movement. "I swear I will never get used to that shit."

"Soon, you'll be able to do it yourself," Papa said with a wink before he disappeared into Scarlette's closet.

"What exactly is going on?" Fallon asked her best friend, who was currently taking the ponytail out of Fallon's hair.

"We are getting you ready for your engagement

party, baby!" Scarlette squealed, no longer able to hold back her excitement.

"Engagement party? When did you guys have time to plan all this? How did you even know I would say yes?" Fallon asked one question after another as she eyed Papa, who came out of Scarlette's closet with a garment bag in his hands.

Scarlette stopped whatever it was she was doing to Fallon's hair and walked around so she could face her. There was an *are you serious* look on her face as she responded to her best friend. "We don't need the ability to foresee the future to know you were going to say yes, Fallon. The way you love Kendrick is obvious as fuck, sis. To answer your other question, you've been in the lab working on your cure so much, we were able to get this shit together easily."

"Yeah," Papa agreed as he laid the dress on Scarlette's bed before taking Fallon's hand and guiding her to the vanity that sat in the corner. "You haven't had time to pay us much attention."

Fallon reached up and patted Papa on the cheek, causing him to give her a lopsided grin, showing his right gold encased fang. "I'm sorry, Papa."

He waved her off. "I'll give you a pass this time, but you know I need attention or I'll perish."

Fallon giggled. "I know, but I have some good news for you."

"And what's that?" Papa asked as he pulled out makeup brushes and selected the eyeshadow pallet he was going to use on Fallon while Scarlette brushed the bride to be's hair. Within the past decade, Papa had become interested in makeup, and he did a phenomenal job at it, too. If he wasn't so hung up on finding a mate, he could have a career in being a makeup artist for celebrities for the next ten years or so.

"I finished the cure, and I want you to be the one to test it out," Fallon said happily.

Papa immediately stopped what he was doing and placed a hand on his chest dramatically. With tears in his eyes, he asked, "Are you serious?"

Fallon grabbed the hand that was clutching his imaginary pearls and caressed it gently. "Of course, I am. I need a test run done to make sure it works, and who better to try it out on than you? My only advice is to make sure you choose someone you actually like. This cure won't technically mate them to you, but it will allow them to survive your bite."

Papa used his free hand to brush the tears streaming down his face away before responding. "I know just the girl. It's perfect. She's coming tonight."

"Papa, are you sure—"

"You'll love her. She's gorgeous, funny, and she

had a bangin' ass body, honey," Papa interrupted Fallon, a dreamy look on his face.

"What's her name?" Fallon asked, knowing Papa had his mind made up already, and there was no way she was going to get him to wait a minute and think about the shit a little longer.

"Sierra," he said whimsically. "We're in love, and tonight will be the perfect night to solidify that love with a bite."

His eyes sparkled, and Fallon shifted in her seat at the half crazed look in her friend's eyes. The man was crazy for love, and Fallon prayed he truly got that out of life soon, because she hated the way his desire was psychologically fucking him up. Papa wasn't a bad vampire. He was just romantically lonely, and being that way for as long as he had was bound to take a toll on anyone. Scarlette was fine being a hoe. She was proud of that shit, and she always said if she met the right one, she would try turning them. Until then, she was having fun. Axel wasn't really pressed about bitches. He had tried turning a few, but he was laid back about love. He figured one day it would come to him. Papa just didn't have that in him. He yearned for deep intimacy.

"I can't wait to meet her," Fallon said kindly. "The

cure is in my bookbag in the foyer. If I forget to grab it for you, feel free to get it yourself."

Papa simply gave her a smile before he went to work on her face, humming quietly and lost in his own little world.

It only took half an hour for the two vampires to get Fallon's face and hair together, and another five minutes for her to slip into her dress and shoes. As she stood in the mirror with her two friends standing behind her, she admired the way she looked. Normally, she put on eyeliner, mascara, and lip gloss. She wasn't used to seeing her face all done up, but the highlighter and red lips made her already dazzling features truly pop. Her ginger hair was curled in wide ringlets and cascading down her shoulders, and the black off the shoulder dress was tasteful and sexy. While she had gotten dressed, Papa and Scarlette had as well. They were both wearing all white and looking good as ever, with little to no effort. Papa let her know that the party was black and white themed, and only she and Kendrick would wear black. They instructed everyone else to wear white.

"Before we go down, I have one more thing to show you," Scarlette said as she squeezed Fallon's shoulders from behind. She disappeared into her closet, and a second later, she emerged with a large garment bag in her hands.

"What's this?" Fallon asked curiously.

"Open it and see," Scarlette said as she laid the bag on the bed.

"You're going to love it," Papa said as he clapped his hands.

Fallon walked over to the bed and unzipped the bag. A gasp fell from her lips as she took in the beautiful white dress.

"I know you've had a lot on your mind, so I decided to get your wedding dress for you. I hope you like it," Scarlette said softly from beside her.

Fallon whirled around and wrapped her arms around her best friend. "It's the most thoughtful thing anyone has ever done for me, Scar. I love it. Thank you."

And Fallon meant it. The dress was made up mostly of lace and looked to be tight fitting with a long train. She couldn't wait to try it on, and almost as if Scarlette was reading her thoughts, she said, "We can try it on tomorrow. First, let's celebrate your engagement the right way."

"Time to get fucked up!" Papa cheered, and the three of them laughed as they exited the room.

Downstairs, guests had filled the entertainment room. Drinks were flowing, and everyone looked so nice dressed up, but Fallon didn't see any of that. Her eyes landed on Kendrick in the sea of people, and she made a beeline for him. His eyes were already on her as soon as she entered the room, so when she was within arm's reach, he pulled her into him and placed a kiss on her lips. "You look beautiful."

Fallon's entire body heated. "You look damn good yourself, Mr. Danger."

He flashed his fangs before licking his lips. "Can I have this dance?"

"Kiss of Life" by Sade was playing softly, and couples were dancing all around them. Fallon had no idea who those people were. She was sure the gang asked random people to come. Since they were so charming and most people couldn't help but become enamored by them, it was easy for them to get humans to do what they wanted, no compulsion ability needed, but that was okay with Fallon. She wasn't paying anyone but her man any attention.

They swayed back and forth for several songs, enjoying the ambiance. It surprised Fallon at how sophisticated the party was, since TFG normally threw wild ass parties that normally resulted in a human or two dead and plenty of Hennessy. This was much classier, and something new for the gang. Fallon appreciated their efforts.

Eventually, their happy bubble was popped when

Papa came over with a petite woman with curves for days. She looked like she was Latina, with long silky hair and dark brown eyes with thick arched brows. "Fal, I wanted you and your future hubby to meet Sierra."

"Hi, Sierra. nice to mee—"

Fallon was cut off when Papa bit Sierra's neck. Fallon held back her scream, so she didn't draw any attention to them. If anyone was looking right now, it would look like Papa was simply kissing on Sierra's neck, but Fallon knew better. She watched in hopeful horror for several long seconds while Papa drained the poor girl of her blood, a look of euphoria on her face. Fallon knew the feeling well. When Kendrick drank from her, it was a feeling like none other. Soon, though, the look of euphoria turned to one of pain. Fallon was guessing it was the pain of her being sucked dry. She had personally never experienced that.

After several long, grueling moments, Papa pulled away from her and said, "Don't worry. I gave her the cure."

With a wink, he looked down at the woman in his arms lovingly, while Fallon stared on in horror. She knew as soon as the last drop of blood was drained from a human after a vampire bite, their heart would immediately stop beating, but if they were mated and starting the turning process, they would continue breathing. The issue here was that Fallon didn't see the rise and fall of Sierra's chest. Dread filled her as Papa seemed to notice the same thing. He held Sierra up in his arms and put his hand over her abdomen and then her chest, feeling for movement.

"No… no, mami. No. What happened?" he asked desperately as he looked between Sierra, who was dead weight in his arms, and Fallon, who immediately felt a great sense of guilt.

"Baby, it's okay," Kendrick whispered in her ear as she watched Papa unravel right before her.

Luckily, before he could cause a scene, Scarlette and Axel appeared. Axel grabbed Sierra from Papa's arms while Scarlette quietly ushered him out of the room.

"I'll take care of her," Axel murmured before taking Sierra's body out of the room, everyone else oblivious as to what just happened.

Fallon watched in a daze before Kendrick stepped into her line of sight and forced her gaze up to him. Her lips trembled as she said, "It didn't work. You knew it wouldn't work… that's why you weren't excited earlier."

Guilt filled Kendrick's eyes. "Shh… baby, it's okay. I won't let anything happen to you, I promise.

The gang and I have already talked about this. We will fight to keep you alive and human if we have to."

Fallon heard what he was saying, but her mind was on Sierra. She didn't even care that he hadn't answered her question. It was because of her that Sierra was now dead. Papa had all the faith in the world in her, and she let them both down. Sierra's blood was on her hands, and she didn't know how she would ever forgive herself. Unfortunately for her, unless she wanted to suffer the same fate as Sierra, she knew she couldn't dwell on this situation. Not now, anyway. She had to get back to the lab, but not tonight. Her engagement party may have been fucked up, but she was going to do her best to enjoy her night with her future husband. Tomorrow, she would take the day off to attend to Papa, and after that, she was on a mission to save her own life.

"FUCK!" Fallon screeched, as she threw a vial across the room. It shattered against the wall at the same time she sank to her knees in defeat. Tears of frustration leaked from her eyes as she used her palms to dig into them to stop the liquid from seeping from her eyes.

The makeshift lab she was in was a complete disaster. It had been exactly twelve days since Sierra's death, and Fallon had been working tirelessly to re-work the cure she created, and that had failed. She was working so much that Kendrick created a lab for her within The Lair, and he hit a lick whenever she needed chemicals and supplies. Fallon had been taking venom from each of the gang as well as blood from herself and them, to try to get the cure right.

Four more times she created a vial of something, and four more times that vial failed her. Papa was losing hope in her. She could feel it, and she didn't blame him. She didn't like that she kept getting his hopes up only for her to fail him time and time again. The blood of five people were now on her hands, and she was slowly going mad. She was at her wit's end and out of time since the wedding was tomorrow. A crazed laugh bubbled to the surface and burst through her lips as she thought about the fact that she was getting married the next day and had no idea where the wedding was even being held. She hadn't a clue about any of the details of the wedding, and it was hers. It was all absurd, and the lack of sleep was getting to her as she fell into a fit of giggles right there in the middle of the room.

Kendrick inched his way into the room. He had heard her outburst and then her laughs from down the hall in their bedroom. When he saw her balled up on the floor, laughing while rocking back and forth, he knew it was time to put an end to all this. Before he could utter a word, she made eye contact with him, and her facial features bunched up.

"And you!" she exclaimed, as if they were in the middle of a conversation. Kendrick knew his baby was losing her shit, and he was prepared to get her mind back right before tomorrow. He watched as she stood to her feet and marched over to him, her finger poked out in front of her. When she was within reach, she poked that finger into his chest. "You Knew every fucking time my so-called *cures* were going to fail. Why wouldn't you tell me beforehand to save me and Papa the heartache, and, oh… I don't know… save some fucking lives?"

"Bae—"

"No!" Fallon screeched, as she slapped his rock-hard abs. "You could have told me, Kendrick. It would have, at the very least, saved us a lot of time."

Kendrick stared down at her and watched as she unraveled in his arms. "You done?" When Fallon didn't respond, he continued. "I know it sounds harsh, baby, but I couldn't tell you, even if it meant sacrificing some lives. I might be able to foresee the outcomes, but I can't always see the *why*. You know this, Beauty. Think about it. The third vial you made kept that girl alive for five hours before she died. I didn't foresee that part. All I saw was that it failed. Had I told you that beforehand, you would have completely discarded that formula, right or wrong?"

Fallon gathered her thoughts for a moment before saying, "Yeah."

"Exactly. Because I let it play out how it needed to. You were able to make an even better formula the next time. Each time they lived longer," Kendrick explained. "Because you had to see that trial and error."

Fallon shook her head sadly. "But they all eventually died, and it was my fault."

"You know as well as I do that Papa would have tried turning those people with or without those cures."

Fallon knew he had a point, but the lack of sleep and the emotional stress she had been under didn't allow her to see that clearly. "I don't give a fu—"

"Aye," Kendrick barked before picking her up and putting her over his shoulder. "Enough taking."

"But—"

Fallon's protests were cut short when Kendrick said, "I said enough, Fallon."

She fell silent for a moment as he walked calmly to their bedroom. When he pushed their door open and sat Fallon on her feet, she tried pushing past him while saying, "Fine, I won't talk, but I need to try one more formula. If I can get it done tonight, Papa can—"

"No," Kendrick said, placing a hand on her chest and stopping her in her tracks.

Fallon looked down at his hand and then up at him. "No?"

He nodded sharply. "Enough is enough, baby. You need to rest. Tomorrow is going to be a big day."

"But—"

"Fallon, baby… stop. Please. You're going to kill yourself if you keep on like this."

Fallon's lower lip trembled, and she looked up at Kendrick with watery eyes. "And what if I die tomorrow?"

Kendrick's face hardened, and his jaws clenched. "You won't."

"You saw it?" Fallon asked, with hope in her eyes.

Kendrick hated to dash away that hope, but he also didn't want to lie to her. "No, Beauty. I still can't see anything about tomorrow. Like I said, it's like there's a block or something because of an outside factor that I can't see. It's driving me insane."

A tear streaked down Fallon's cheek. "Then how do you know I won't die?"

"Because I won't allow it. You still want to marry me, right? You can leave tonight—"

"No, Kendrick. No. I want to marry you," Fallon cut him off. And she truly did. Even though she hadn't been much help in the wedding planning, the idea of a wedding dangling in her face had her wide open. She didn't realize how badly she wanted to marry Kendrick until that very moment. Until the idea of it being snatched away from her was presented the day before it was supposed to happen, even if it meant she would have to get bitten. She would rather die Kendrick's wife than live without him.

Kendrick pushed a stray strand of her wild hair out of her face and behind her ear before saying, "Okay, then. Tonight, you rest. That's final."

Fallon wanted to go against the grain, but her body was tired. She was exhausted, and she knew Kendrick was right. She needed to rest up and prepare for whatever was going to happen the next day.

Kendrick could sense the moment Fallon gave in to him, so he scooped her up in his arms and put her right in bed before stripping her of her black sweatpants and matching hoodie. She was left only in her black lace bra and thong. Kendrick couldn't help it… he looked at her with lust in his eyes.

"I thought the bride and groom weren't supposed to see each other before the wedding, Mr. Danger," Fallon said softly when she noticed the look in Kendrick's eyes.

"Fuck all that," Kendrick responded before he quickly took his own clothes off and got into bed beside her, tugging at her panties and then her bra.

They stared into each other's eyes for a moment before Kendrick leaned over and kissed her. "Let me put you to sleep."

"I don't think it'll take much," Fallon murmured

against his lips. She could feel sleep pulling at her while her mind slowly shut down. She desperately wanted to latch on to the thoughts about the wedding, the cure… anything productive, but her brain felt scrambled, and it was simply impossible. Instead, she focused on Kendrick, who was now kissing on her neck. She moaned before she realized it had been several days since he'd fed off her. "Baby, I'm sorry. You haven't had any blood—"

"Don't be sorry. We've both been preoccupied," he said, cutting her off.

"That's no excuse." Fallon sighed before tugging on his arm.

Kendrick took the hint and adjusted himself so he was nestled between her legs, his hard dick at her slippery opening. Fallon covered her mouth to yawn, and Kendrick chuckled. "A quickie it is."

"Please," Fallon breathed, before wrapping her arms around his neck and pulling him to her for a kiss. Their tongues intertwined at the same time he entered her. Fallon gasped before moaning in pleasure. "I missed you."

"I missed you too, Beauty," Kendrick replied as he gave her long, slow strokes.

Fallon was delirious with sleepiness and pleasure. His dick working in and out of her was feeling so damn good, and it was the only thing keeping her awake. "Baby…"

"I know. Let it go, baby," Kendrick responded, close to an orgasm himself.

He felt Fallon tightening around his dick, and he knew she was about to make a mess. Timing it perfectly, he kissed her neck sensually before latching on and biting her, just with the very tips of his fangs.

Fallon cried out and arched her back, and Kendrick looked down at the small pool of blood on her neck. He licked his lips hungrily before suctioning his lips around where he bit and sucking. She tasted so damn good to him. He would bite her every hour if he could, but he controlled his urges because he didn't want to drain her. The most he had bitten her was three times in a day, and even that was overdoing it.

He drank his fill while Fallon came all over his dick. He came with her as he watched her face contort into a beautiful frame of ecstasy. Her mind was in a state of euphoria, and as soon as he pulled away and kissed her neck, she had forgotten completely what had just happened, but because she knew about vampires and could easily recognize the tingling sensation all over her body, she was able to put two and two together.

"Did you get enough?" she asked as she reached up to feel her neck.

Kendrick smirked as he came down from his own orgasmic high. He knew she remembered nothing about being bitten, and the small amount of venom that entered her system already healed the bite mark he left behind, but she always seemed to know when he had bitten her, anyway. He had met humans who knew about vampires and got bitten often, but never knew afterward. Fallon, however, was different. He chalked it up to her being too damn smart for her own good.

"More than enough. Rest now, Beauty."

Fallon snuggled up to him and said, "I love you, Kendrick."

"I love you too, Fallon." He wanted to reassure her again about tomorrow, but she was already fast asleep, and that was okay with him because truth be told, he had no idea what the fuck tomorrow would bring, and the shit was bothering him more than he would ever let on.

"GOOD! YOU'RE AWAKE!" Scarlette chirped as she barged into Fallon's room with her long hair in a messy bun and nothing but a long t-shirt on.

Fallon had just opened her eyes one second before Scarlette came through the doors. She sat up with one eye open because the light from the window was entirely too bright. "Barely. What time is it?"

Fallon looked to the side of her and noticed Kendrick was no longer in bed. She knew she had been sleeping extra hard if she hadn't even felt him get up.

"I let you sleep as long as possible, babe, but we have to get up and moving. The ceremony is in three hours," Scarlette replied as she pulled the covers from Fallon's body, not even giving her naked body a second glance.

Fallon covered herself with the sheet and looked

at Scarlette, alarmed. "Three hours? Oh my God! How could you guys let me sleep that long?"

Panic filled Fallon as she jumped out of bed and rushed into her closet to find something to wear. The weight of what today would bring rested heavily on her shoulders. She couldn't believe she had slept so late on today of all days.

Scarlette was in the huge walk-in closet before Fallon could touch an article of clothing. She turned Fallon around to face her, while Fallon used her hands to cover her breasts and pussy.

"Chill," Scarlette demanded. "Everything is under control."

"How is it under control, Scarlette? I might die today!" Fallon screeched with tears in her eyes.

Scarlette shook her head. "No. You won't die today, sis. We have it all planned out. After the wedding ceremony, we are going to run. I already have your bags packed with the shit that's important to you. It's waiting in one of Kendrick's cars. We got you."

Fallon shook her head with wide eyes. "Wh... what are you talking about? We can't run. Prima and Maximus won't allow that—"

"They don't have a say, Fallon. We have it all planned out. All you have to do is get married and look pretty. Let the vamps do the rest."

"Why not just leave now, then? I don't get it…" Fallon said, the panic she felt when she woke up rising and spreading through her entire body. Being on the run from Prima and Maximus didn't exactly feel like an ideal happy ending, nor her ideal honeymoon. She wished the gang had consulted her about this first because she wasn't sure this was something she wanted to do. Of course, getting bit without knowing if she would survive or not wasn't the ideal alternative.

Scarlette sat down at the plush bench in the middle of the closet and tugged Fallon down to sit beside her. "Because, bestie… this wedding is important. Plus, they're footing the bill."

Fallon laughed incredulously. "Seriously?"

"Dead serious, sweetie. I mean, I'm joking about the money part, but the wedding is happening today. Kendrick was set on having the wedding. I think it's more important to y'all than you two have admitted to even yourselves, so just enjoy the day. Leave everything else up to us."

Fallon cleared her throat to get rid of the lump that was forming there. She took a deep breath and nodded her head. "It's my wedding day," she whispered.

Scarlette's face cracked into a smile. "It is, baby girl."

Fallon thought about her grandmother at that moment, and she was sad. She and her grandmother had a great relationship until she turned eighteen and met Kendrick. Things got rocky to the point that her grandmother kicked her out of her house, and Fallon hadn't seen or heard from her grandmother since. Regret at how things unfolded between them filled her, but she mentally pushed those thoughts away so she could focus on the positive. "I guess we have a wedding to get ready for."

Scarlette looped her arm through Fallon's and walked toward the bedroom. "That, we do."

Fallon stopped in her tracks and said, "Uh, Scar… mind if I wash my ass and put some clothes on first?"

Scarlette turned around and looked Fallon up and down. "Good idea."

Fallon giggled before making her way to the bathroom, looking forward to a moment alone before the day ahead of her.

TWO AND A HALF HOURS LATER, Fallon was standing in front of the full-length mirror in her room, while Scarlette stood behind her with tears in her eyes. Fallon grinned, blinking away tears herself. "What's wrong, gang?"

Scarlette let out a high-pitched laugh. "Bitch, bye. You know I can be sentimental sometimes, or whatever."

Fallon let out a giggle. "This I know, but don't start crying because then I will, and then I'll probably have a panic attack… and all your hard work will have been in vain."

"Can't have that," Scarlette said, waving her hand in front of her face to stop her tears. "I'm just so happy for you, sis."

Fallon gave her a small smile. "Let's hope your guys' plan works so that happiness is justified."

"Hey," Scarlette said, lifting Fallon's chin so their green eyes could link. "Everything is going to be fine. Now, take a moment to yourself, but don't sit down, don't cry, and don't touch your hair or face."

"Anything else?" Fallon asked playfully.

Scarlette slapped her on the butt before walking toward the door. "Don't panic."

"Got it," Fallon said with a wink, before Scarlette walked out of the room, closing the door behind her so she could get herself ready before the ceremony, which would be held right there at The Lair. Prima thought it would be more convenient for the biting ceremony, something she had completely made up and was making a big fuss over.

When she was left alone, she turned her gaze back to the mirror and smiled. The rule of the afternoon had been no boys allowed, which was why Scarlette didn't enlist Papa to do her makeup to save some time. Scarlette did Fallon's nails, makeup, and hair, and she did a phenomenal job. She barely even looked like herself, yet she did. She looked elegant, and the dress she wore had been modified to fit her taste, which was another surprise from Scarlette. She had taken the time to replace some of the white lace through the tight fitting dress with black lace. The dress was still predominately white, but the black made it unique and made Fallon feel more comfortable. She had never been much of a girly girl, but she was damn sure sexy, and this dress did it for her. It dipped low in the front and the back, while the trail flared out at the back just below her plump ass. It was perfect. Her hair was in an intricate updo, and the black and white rose bouquet set everything off perfectly.

While she was admiring herself in the mirror, the bedroom door slowly opened, and Fallon's smile broadened. For a moment, she thought Kendrick had snuck in to see her, but her smile faltered when a man she didn't know stepped into the room. He closed the door behind him and finally looked directly at her, piercing her soul with his dark eyes. Fallon stayed frozen in place. She didn't feel threatened by the man, but his presence confused her. The more she stared at him, the more he seemed familiar to her, but she couldn't ever remember seeing him before. She squinted her emerald eyes at him and said, "I'm sorry… do I know you?"

"Fallon Bordeaux," the man said in a baritone voice.

The way he said her name caused chills to run down her spine. He spoke softly, almost as if he wasn't trying to be heard. She noticed the sides of his head were shaved, like Kendrick's, but the dreads on top of his head were much longer and sitting neatly in a bun at the top of his head. There was a dangling cross earring in his left earlobe, and both sides of his nose were pierced. The suit he wore covered the tattoos peeking out from under the black sleeves, and Fallon was willing to bet he was covered in them.

"Are you asking?" she asked cautiously as she looked around the room, looking for a weapon. She still didn't feel threatened, but she wasn't sure of the stranger's intentions.

He chuckled, and Fallon's heart kicked up. "Nah, baby. I know exactly who you are."

"How—"

She stopped talking because one moment he was across the room and the next he was standing directly in front of her, grasping her chin firmly in his hand. Her eyes grew wide because she realized he was a vampire, and that made her slightly more nervous, but as she gazed into the stranger's eyes, she felt at ease. She wondered if he knew Kendrick, and she was about to ask, but he spoke first.

"You look beautiful."

She shivered again, and a crooked grin graced his face, reminding her so much of Kendrick. She was about to ask him if he and her future husband were related when he said, "We got company," before kissing her cheek gently and disappearing. Fallon noticed her closet door closing gently, and she figured that was where the stranger had disappeared before her bedroom door opened, and Prima walked in, followed by Maximus.

Now, Fallon was completely uneasy, because the sinister grins they wore told her something bad was about to happen, and she was the only one in the room, aside from a strange man she didn't know who was hiding in the closet.

"OH, don't worry, darling. Kendrick should be here in a moment," Prima stated when she saw the look of unease on Fallon's face.

"I compelled one of the humans to tell him to meet us up here in exactly one minute," Maximus chimed in.

Fallon swallowed the lump in her throat. "I thought it was bad luck for the groom to see the bride before the wedding?"

She was nervous and desperately trying to figure out what the king and queen wanted with her. She had a feeling they were about to shake shit up, and her heart pounded in anticipation.

"We don't believe in that," Prima said, waving her hand in dismissal.

"Believe in what?" Kendrick asked as he walked into the room. Fallon's breath caught when she saw him. He had a black tux on with a black vest and black button-up shirt. His hair was freshly lined, and his dreads were twisted neatly at the top of his head. He was at her side before his mother could respond to his question, gathering Fallon in his arms. "You look stunning, Beauty."

Fallon's cheeks warmed, and for a moment, she forgot about his parents being in the room. She reached up and caressed his face lovingly. "I can't believe I'm about to be your wife."

"About that," Prima cut in. "We have a change of plans."

Kendrick immediately turned so his back was to Fallon, and he was facing his parents. "What do you mean?"

"We thought it would be ridiculous to host a wedding for you two if Fallon would not survive your bite, so we postponed the wedding. You'll bite her now, and if she survives, we will have the wedding when she wakes up," Prima said with a smile on her face, as if she had just delivered good news.

A cold sweat broke out on Fallon's forehead as her heart drummed in her ears. She knew today was going entirely too smoothly. The gut feeling she had when she woke up… that panic that had started her day… that shit had been warranted. She had a flash of anger toward Scarlette, and even Kendrick, for giving her false hope, but she realized it wasn't entirely their fault. Kendrick may have had the ability of foresight, but he was adamant that there was some kind of block on the day, preventing him from seeing any sort of outcome.

"What about the guests downstairs?" Kendrick asked. "I was just down there, and everything is ready to go. We might as well go through with the original plan."

Fallon could feel Kendrick's worry, but he covered it up with ease. She reached out and touched his tense back, hoping to provide a source of comfort. If she was going to potentially die within the next few minutes, she wanted to feel him, to soak in as much of him as she possibly could.

"I compelled them to stay for as long as we need them," Maximus said with a grand smile as if he had done them a huge favor. "Hopefully she will turn quickly, and it won't take days."

Kendrick gritted his teeth. "No."

Prima lifted an arched brow and took a step closer to her son. "No?"

"No. I will not go along with this. If I am going to bite her, at the very least you can let me marry her first," Kendrick tried to reason.

"Or I can make you bite her," Maximus countered, and in a flash, Prima had Kendrick held against her, his back to her chest, and her hand at his throat.

"Stop wasting our time, Kendrick, and bite her," Prima said menacingly.

"Mother, why are you doing this?" Kendrick asked, and Fallon could see the pain in his face. Whenever he used to talk about his parents, it was with a distant sort of love. She knew he cared deeply for them, but she could also understand why he tried keeping away from them. They weren't the most loving parents, and Fallon was seeing that unfold right before her eyes.

"You are a king, son. You are meant to rule. We are the original vampires, Kendrick. Do you know what that means? It means you need to find a mate so you can take your proper seat on the throne," Prima replied.

"Listen to your mother, son. We can do this the easy way, or the hard way. The choice is yours," Maximus said while looking at his son with hard features.

Tears were now streaming down Fallon's face, and she wanted to reassure Kendrick that it was okay. He was outnumbered, and she certainly wouldn't be any help in a fight. Their eyes connected, and Fallon mouthed, *it's okay. I love you.*

Kendrick shook his head, but before he could even try to make a move to get him and the love of his life out of this mess, the closet door opened, and there was an audible gasp from the three other vampires in the room.

The stranger strolled into the bedroom, looking cocky as hell while circling Fallon. He looked at her while speaking to everyone else. "Actually, Mother, I believe that throne belongs to me."

Mother? Fallon thought.

"How the fuck is this even possible? I thought we took care of him—"

"Almost a thousand years ago? Ah, yes. You *thought* you took care of me, Brother." The man cut Kendrick off, and Fallon took in a shocked breath. *Brother?* No wonder he looked familiar to her. He was Kendrick's brother. The resemblance was definitely there, but Fallon could sense the differences in them. Kendrick was calm and reasonable… his brother… she could sense pain within him, and that made him dangerous, but dangerous or not, Fallon wasn't afraid. She didn't feel the need to be.

"Remington, you're supposed to be somewhere in the Antarctic," Maximus said, his voice booming. Fallon sensed a sliver of worry coming from him, which she found odd.

"I spent a century there, and I have to admit, it

was hell, but it was also by choice. Funny thing, though. You all never stopped to wonder what my ability was. You all have them. Did you think I wouldn't?" Remington asked, as he continued looking Fallon up and down. "No matter. The point is… I've been keeping tabs on you all through the years, but I've kept my distance. When I heard my little brother was getting married, I had to make an appearance."

"You aren't welcome here," Kendrick snarled, and he pushed back at his mother, who still held him. She had an iron grip on him, though. Any time he tried to push away from her, she gripped him tighter.

"This is a family meeting, isn't it? Am I not a part of the family? I think I belong here as much as you all." He finally stopped looking at Fallon and made eye contact with each member of his family. "What is the topic of discussion? Ms. Bordeaux?"

"Get the fuck out," Kendrick snapped. "Go back to keeping yo' distance, nigga. I promise it's what's best because once Mother let's me go, I'ma kill yo' ass for even speaking my wife's name."

Remington laughed, and another chill went through Fallon's body while she watched the brothers go at it. "Sorry, baby bro… I'm not going anywhere. In fact, I've decided to stick around. Now, here's my input. I vote on turning Fallon."

"Nigga, you don't get a vote," Kendrick barked.

Maximus held his hand up and said, "Are you willing to help us get your brother to bite her, son?"

Remington walked up to his father and stood toe to toe with him. "I ain't your son, nigga. You lost the privilege of addressing me as such when you left me for dead." He looked at his mother. "Same goes for you."

"Then what are you doing here, Remington? You're supposed to be dead, for fuck's sake. Why show up now?" Prima asked, exasperated.

Remington laughed, and the tension in the room grew. Fallon made eye contact with Kendrick once again. She felt helpless, and Kendrick hated to see her like that. As a last ditch effort, he mouthed, *run*. He knew she could never outrun the vampires, but it could provide a distraction so he could hopefully get them out of this mess.

Fallon did as she was told, and made a move toward the door, but Remington caught her effortlessly in his strong arms. "I'll answer your question first, Prima. I'm here because you have something I want." He turned to his father. "And to answer your previous question, Maximus, no. I won't help you to get Kendrick to bite Fallon. I'll do you one better."

Without warning, Fallon felt fangs sink into her

neck. Euphoria overtook her as she heard Kendrick scream, "No!"

She wanted to go to him, but she felt too good to move. It wasn't long, though, before pain overtook her. She cringed and tried pulling away when she felt a searing pain overtake her body. She wanted to scream, but she was stuck in place while Remington sucked her dry. The last thing she saw was Kendrick, with tears in his eyes and calling her name, before everything went black.

To be continued...

CYN'S CATALOG

Get signed copies at: Cynful Monarch

SERIES:

The Urban Fairytales Series (Complete Collection - all books in 1): https://amzn.to/2V7rk6d

Dust to Diamonds (Book 1 of the Urban Fairytale Series): https://amzn.to/3rT9srt

The Baddest of Them All (Book 2 of the Urban Fairytale Series): https://amzn.to/3lnnSyU

Lil Red Ryder (Book 3 of the Urban Fairytale Series): https://amzn.to/3xoLbKV

Rebel & Her Beast (Book 4 of the Urban Fairytale Series): https://amzn.to/3ih5kyr

A Fairytale Wedding (Book 5 of the Urban Fairytale Series): https://amzn.to/3rQ6O63

The Princess & the Goon (Spin-off of the Urban Fairytale Series): https://amzn.to/3fkDmQf

Billion Dollar Baddie: https://amzn.to/37cGVnr

Billion Dollar Baddie 2: https://amzn.to/3A4GRCm

Anything for the Family: https://amzn.to/3CcdvEi

Anything for the Family 2: https://amzn.to/3w0oqyt

Lux Rose: https://amzn.to/3wuib6e

Lux Rose 2: https://amzn.to/3MrZlCJ

Lux Rose 3: https://amzn.to/3Roq9re

STANDALONES:

Baby, it's Cold Outside: https://amzn.to/2V7ZSoX

The Married Woman: https://amzn.to/33k9jp1

A Hood Chick's Savior: https://amzn.to/3ykaAHf

Hell Hath No Fury: Beaten at your Own Game: https://amzn.to/3FmZRyE

COLLABS:

Bosses Link Up: https://amzn.to/37d2292

Endlessly Mine: https://amzn.to/3n0bwfk

<u>VELLA STORIES:</u>

A Hood Chick's Outlaw: https://amzn.to/3rNjdYh

LET'S CONNECT!

Join my readers group on Facebook, and stay up on
all releases, get character visuals and sneak peeks,
and even get in on giveaways!
https://www.facebook.com/groups/
277463019954112/

Sign up for my email list! Get exclusive content and
discounts!
https://bit.ly/39tvXOC

Hey There!

Thank you for your support on my literary journey. I hope your reading experience was a pleasant one. Please leave a review on Goodreads and Amazon. Please feel free to connect with me to stay current on upcoming releases and reader specific exclusives.